S0-EAQ-731

## "YOU DON'T KNOV [S0-EAQ-731] I'VE WISHED YOU WERE HERE WITH ME," GRADY SAID HUSKILY.

Jennie's eyes met his and she felt the shock of his gaze burning into her. "Now I'm here," she said unsteadily, and slowly he lowered his lips to her sensuously parted ones. Her breath caught in her throat as his hand cupped her breast, his strong fingers beginning to unloosen the buttons of her shirt.

"Jennie Winters, you are a beautiful woman," he murmured when his lips finally parted from hers. "I want you so badly . . ."

Staring into the stormy cauldron of his eyes, Jennie realized the decision was hers to make. She must either stop here or not stop at all. And she knew she wanted this man as much as he wanted her . . .

---

KATHERINE RANSOM held various jobs, including computer programming, before becoming a full-time writer. She loves antiques, American folk art, and visiting Cape Cod. She lives in Connecticut, and is the president of the local Romance Writers of America there.

Dear Reader:

The editors of Rapture Romance have only one thing to say—thank you! At a time when there are so many books to choose from, you have welcomed ours with open arms, trying new authors, coming back again and again, and writing to us of your enthusiasm. Frankly, we're thrilled!

In fact, the response has been so great that we now feel confident that you are ready for more stories which explore all the possibilities that exist when today's men and women fall in love. We are proud to announce that we will now be publishing six titles each month, because you've told us that four Rapture Romances simply aren't enough. Of course, we won't substitute quantity for quality! We will continue to select only the finest of sensual love stories, stories in which the passionate physical expression of love is the glorious culmination of the entire experience of falling in love.

And please keep writing to us! We love to hear from our readers, and we take your comments and opinions seriously. If you have a few minutes, we would appreciate your filling out the questionnaire at the back of this book, or feel free to write us at the address below. Some of our readers have asked how they can write to their favorite authors, and we applaud their thoughtfulness. Writers need to hear from their fans, and while we cannot give out addresses, we are more than happy to forward any mail.

Happy reading!

Robin Grunder
Rapture Romance
New American Library
1633 Broadway
New York, NY 10019

# O'HARA'S WOMAN

by
Katherine Ransom

A SIGNET BOOK

NEW AMERICAN LIBRARY

TIMES MIRROR

*PUBLISHER'S NOTE*

This novel is a work of fiction. Names, characters, places, and incidents either are the product of the author's imagination or are used fictitiously, and any resemblance to actual persons, living or dead, events, or locales is entirely coincidental.

NAL BOOKS ARE AVAILABLE AT QUANTITY DISCOUNTS
WHEN USED TO PROMOTE PRODUCTS OR SERVICES.
FOR INFORMATION PLEASE WRITE TO PREMIUM MARKETING DIVISION,
THE NEW AMERICAN LIBRARY, INC., 1633 BROADWAY,
NEW YORK, NEW YORK 10019.

Copyright © 1983 by Mary Fanning Sederquest

All rights reserved

SIGNET, SIGNET CLASSIC, MENTOR, PLUME, MERIDIAN and NAL BOOKS
are published by The New American Library, Inc.,
1633 Broadway, New York, New York 10019

First Printing, November, 1983

1  2  3  4  5  6  7  8  9

PRINTED IN THE UNITED STATES OF AMERICA

*To Amy Lines-Doherty
and my parents and Ed—
who were with me when I needed them*

# Chapter One

"I want it."

Jennie Winters stood with her hands on her slim hips, her long brunette hair tied back with a red ribbon. In her trim designer jeans and T-shirt with a famous emblem she looked more like a teenager than a thirty-two-year-old insurance executive. She turned her brown, gold-flecked eyes to the real-estate agent and repeated her words: "I want it. It's perfect."

Gladys Peevy, fifty-five and resigned to the world, shrugged. "It's pretty dilapidated."

Jennie smiled with unconcern. She saw in her mind's eye how it would look when she was finished with it: a red-painted clapboard building with brick steps leading up to the white door, sparkling twelve-over-twelve windows shining in the sun, and flowers massed along the stone wall that fronted the property. The knee-high tangle of grass and weeds would become a smooth green carpet over which the two towering maples would throw their gentle, dappled shade.

She inhaled the sweet scent of clover, wildflowers, and wild mint that mingled with the smell of freshly mown hay from a field just down the road. Tilting her head to stare up through the spreading branches of the maple, she could glimpse the brilliant blue sky. Occasional puffy white clouds floated by, like small rafts on a calm sea.

She inhaled again and felt the quiet seep into her city-bred bones, felt the sweet peace that follows a decision well made, and knew she had found her weekend home. "This is it," she said, throwing Mrs. Peevy a quiet smile. "It feels like home already."

"The owner," Mrs. Peevy said once they got back to her office and she had checked the multiple-listing book, "is Dana Avery." Gladys Peevy peered up at Jennie over her half-moon-shaped glasses. "Dana's family owned almost all the land in eastern Connecticut a hundred or so years ago. Dana still owns quite a bit around Stockton. That old place has been on the market almost two years. It was listed with another agency and I've never shown it before, that's why I'm not too familiar with it. Shall I call him and see if he can see us now? You might be able to pick that place up pretty cheap—as I say, it's been on the market quite a while."

Jennie smiled serenely. "Yes, let's see if he can meet with us now. Then I'll try to find a local carpenter this afternoon to go over it with me."

Privately she knew that even if a carpenter told her the schoolhouse was falling down with termites, she would still buy it. It had reached out to her much the way her kitten, Ragamuffin, had at the Humane Society a few years back. She had never regretted getting Muffie on the spur of the moment, and she knew instinctively that she wouldn't regret buying this place.

Gladys Peevy reached for the phone, then hesitated. "Of course, the cost of renovating that place could really add up, you realize, Miss Winters. You could end up paying more for it than you would for a place that's already been restored, or even a newer place."

Jennie's generous mouth curved into a warm smile. "I've been looking for a weekend home for over a month, combing every part of Connecticut and the Berkshires. *This* is what I want, Mrs. Peevy. There's just something about it . . ." She flashed an almost embarrassed look at the older woman. "Anyway, it will be fun to fix it up, to see it change before my eyes—like making a dream come true."

Jennie looked away from those knowing eyes, feeling like a child chastised for dreaming. But then her chin rose a fraction of an inch and her gold-flecked eyes became just slightly stern. She was *determined* to buy that schoolhouse. It might be a foolish dream to Gladys Peevy, but for Jennie it was a chance to live again, to feel excitement coursing through her veins.

Jennie knew Mrs. Peevy had taken her for a tenderfoot, out for a lark in the country, with stars in her eyes and too much money in her pocketbook. The older woman probably thought Jennie didn't realize the work that would have to go into that dilapidated property. But Jennie wasn't afraid of hard work—it had gotten her to her present position at TransContinental Insurance in Hartford. She was the youngest woman officer in the company and she hadn't achieved that by sleeping her way there, by playing on her good looks, or by fooling anyone about her ability. She had earned her place in the hierarchy. When she went to the dining room where the other officers ate, she knew she belonged.

But now she was getting used to her work. Time was hanging heavy on her hands, and there was just so much overtime she could put in. Weekends were beginning to be a chore rather than a reward for a week of hard work. And so she had settled on the idea of buying a weekend place, somewhere within an hour or two of Hartford where she could escape on Friday afternoons and not have to return until Monday, when she could throw herself into her work once more.

When Mrs. Peevy had made the appointment with Dana Avery, the two women rose from their chairs and walked out of the office toward Gladys Peevy's car.

With her old gnarled hand on the door handle, Gladys glanced over at Jennie. "I still say that little Cape I showed you this morning is a better deal. It's sound as a dollar, clean as a whistle, and neat as a pin."

Jennie couldn't resist adding with an impish grin, "And dull as a doorknob."

For the first time, Gladys Peevy seemed to respond to Jennie. Eyeing her up and down, she grinned. "You have a mind of your own, don't you, Miss Winters?"

"Yes," Jennie said. "I definitely have a mind of my own."

Pulling open the car door, Gladys heaved her sagging body into the car. "Well," she said, sounding almost grudging, "you just might fit in around here. Yes," she mused. "You just might."

Dana Avery's home turned out to be one of the gracious white clapboard Colonials that lined the village green of Stockton. But whereas some of the other homes lining the green showed signs of peeling paint and rusty hinges, Dana Avery's home was trim and neat and shining, everything showing the meticulous care that only sufficient money can ensure.

The double doors stood open, admitting the late-morning sunshine into the wide central hall. A lowboy sat near the gracefully curving staircase, and a bowl of day lilies reflected in the antique mirror mounted on the wall over it.

"Dana?" Gladys Peevy yelled through the screen door. "You home?"

There was silence for a moment, then the sound of footsteps bounding down the stairs two at a time. A teenage girl appeared in the doorway and grinned at the two women. "Hi, Mrs. Peevy. Dad's outside on the terrace. Come on in and I'll bring you out back." The young girl's eyes glanced speculatively toward Jennie, then skittered away.

"How're you doing, Lucy?" Gladys asked, following the slim girl through the hall toward another screen door at the back of the house. "Enjoying your vacation?"

Lucy looked back and grinned over her shoulder. "Am I! I just hope the summer goes a lot slower than the rest of the year! I'm so sick of school I could scream!"

Jennie smiled to herself. The girl appeared to be about sixteen, a pretty, healthy-looking, all-American typed with blond hair and blue eyes and good long legs that gave her a kind of coltish grace. Her figure was firm and trim and Jennie thought that there must be more than one boy in town with a crush on her.

"Dad?" Lucy Avery swung open the screen door and strode onto the brick terrace. "Mrs. Peevy's here." She looked back and eyed Jennie doubtfully. "And that customer . . ."

Dana Avery stood up slowly and Jennie stopped thinking about his daughter. He was a tall man, with light brown hair that tumbled into his blue eyes. His face was tanned, his eyes pleasant as he approached Gladys Peevy, but he seemed to notice only Jennie. He wore white tennis shorts which showed his tanned legs and a white T-shirt with the same famous emblem that Jennie's shirt had on hers.

In that split second, Jennie recognized him as one of "her" kind of men. At work, he would wear a three-piece suit and a rep tie with an Oxford button-down shirt. He would be pleasant, well-educated, and able to talk easily with almost anyone at a party. He would also know the correct wines to order at a good restaurant, and would probably, from the looks of his trim body, be quite a good sportsman.

In short, he was like half a dozen other men who had briefly figured in her life during the past fifteen years. He was like the hundreds who crowded the corridors of TransContinental Insurance during lunch. He was familiar, steady, and unthreatening. Jennie smiled at him and felt herself relax. She'd be able to hold her own with him in business negotiations, and would probably be able to manage a discreet involvement with him afterward. . . .

Then her mind skittered away from that possibility. That was the problem with her life—too much of the same thing all the time. She needed a change. That's why she'd decided to buy a weekend retreat. About a year ago she had realized that the men she was dating were all cut from the same mold, and so she had stopped dating. The past year hadn't been so bad—lonely at times, but still, all in all, she had coped with it pretty well. She didn't want to let herself become interested in

Dana Avery as a person. He owned the property she wanted to buy. Let it remain that way.

But Dana Avery seemed to be thinking along opposite lines. His blue eyes had inspected her quite carefully and the handshake he gave her when Gladys Peevy introduced them was slightly longer than convention required.

"So you're interested in the old schoolhouse," he said when they had settled into lawn chairs and iced tea had been poured.

"Yes," Jennie said, meeting his eyes directly. "It's a mess, of course, but I think it has possibilities."

He grinned at her. "I'm glad somebody finally realized that. It's been on the market almost two years now and I'm tired of trying to keep it up. I haven't had anyone go over there to mow the grass or do any repairs at all this year, so you're seeing it at a disadvantage. The setting is really quite nice. No other houses for about a mile."

Jennie nodded, sipping at her tea. "I can see beyond the overgrown weeds, Mr. Avery," she said quietly. "Just what are you asking for it and how much land is there?"

"It's just about three acres," he answered. "All good land, bordered by that old stone wall. There's a well, but no running water or electricity in the place." He glanced at her speculatively. "It would take quite a lot of renovation."

She smiled. Everyone in Stockton seemed to be concerned that she realize just how much work would have to go into the restoration of the old place. "What are you asking, Mr. Avery?" she prompted gently.

He hesitated, then answered. "Forty-nine, nine."

"For that?" Jennie wanted to whoop with laughter. "For three acres and a dilapidated building?"

Nonplussed, Dana Avery stared at her, then he set down his glass of iced tea and shifted in his chair. Jennie smiled to herself. So. He was just beginning to recognize that she wasn't just some fluffy-headed female ready to be bilked.

"The land is quite good land, Miss Winters," he said, sounding slightly stuffy. "You'll not find a nicer piece of property in northeastern Connecticut. The location is good—we're quite close to the Massachusetts border and Sturbridge and yet we're very rural. It's peaceful. There's good fresh air. And I take it that you've recognized the beauty of the old building and can see its potential, so I don't think my price is unreasonable."

"Thirty-five thousand, even," Jennie said firmly, and noticed that Gladys Peevy's eyebrows shot up. Lucy Avery was staring hard at the brick terrace under her sneakered feet, her face unreadable. Dana Avery was smiling at her.

"How like a woman," he said softly, "not to know the value of land. Gladys, you really must take Miss Winters in hand and teach her about real-estate values these days."

Jennie felt as if she had been stung by a bee. Her chin went up and her golden eyes glittered warningly. She hadn't liked that comment about her being "just like a woman." There had been something condescending about it, and no one condescended to Jennie. No one.

"What will you take, Mr. Avery?" she asked, her voice no longer quite as warm as it had been. "I assure you, after spending the last few weeks combing the countryside for a place, I'm well aware of the value of real estate."

"Oh . . . I might come down five thousand," he said, his eyes scanning the sky overhead.

"Forty thousand," Jennie countered. "And that's my final offer."

He lowered his eyes and studied her awhile, seeming to take her measure. Briefly his eyes fluttered away; then he smiled and nodded at Jennie. "That might be possible. I'll have to think it over."

"And so will I, Mr. Avery," she said. "I'll need to inspect the place thoroughly, go over it with a carpenter." She glanced at Gladys Peevy. "Can you recommend anyone from around here, Mrs. Peevy?"

Gladys Peevy pursed her lips and sat thinking. "Well," she answered finally, "there are lots of good carpenters and contractors around. Real estate's slow now, you understand, so many of them are practically begging for work." She nodded to herself then and said, "But you should probably see Grady O'Hara. That's such an old building you're looking at, you'll want an expert, someone who really knows what he's doing. That'd be Grady. Wouldn't you agree, Dana?"

"He's about the best around," he agreed. "He's done good work for me."

Gladys nodded and continued. "Grady does a lot of colonial restoration around here. He used to work up at Sturbridge Village in Massachusetts as some kind of expert, but he left to work on his own a few years back. He's a good man. And he knows old buildings. I've seen him dismantle an old house board by board, number each one, and then move each piece a good twenty miles and put the whole thing back together again."

Gladys Peevy's face became animated as she warmed to her subject. "Regular magician with houses, that man look passed between them.

Jennie saw Dana Avery smile at Glayds' words as a

"Difficult?" she asked cautiously. "In what way?"

Dana Avery sat unmoving, not about to answer. Mrs. Peevy mulled over her words before replying. "Well, Grady's his own man. Very independent. Doesn't like to be interfered with. He lives alone in an old saltbox he restored—as a matter of fact, it's not too far from that old schoolhouse. He did all the work by hand. He's a craftsman, as I say, but . . ." Her words trailed off and she shrugged. "Well, you can see for yourself when you meet him. Some people take to Grady like ducks to water. Others can't abide him. It's like I say—he's his own man. If he wants something, he goes after it. If he thinks he's right, he's adamant. Won't budge."

"Stubborn." Jennie supplied the word.

Mrs. Peevy considered that. "Well, stubborn' is a negative word, isn't it, now? And I don't mean to imply that Grady's not a good man. Personally, I like him a lot. He's just got his convictions, is all, and he stands by them, come hell or high water."

Jennie glanced at Dana Avery. "Do you agree, Mr. Avery?"

He flashed her a charming smile. "I agree with your first impression, Miss Winters—Grady's just plain stubborn."

In that instant, Jennie thought she saw a flash of male rivalry. Dana Avery, it appeared, wasn't the kind of man who was going to say anything praiseworthy about any other man, especially to a woman. Jennie filed that bit of knowledge about him in her mind and stood up.

"Thanks so much for the iced tea, Mr. Avery," she said, holding out her hand. "It was nice meeting you, Lucy."

Startled, the teenager looked up and smiled stiffly. She nodded and looked back down at her feet, but not before her guileless blue eyes had studied every inch of Jennie Winters.

Back in the car, heading for Mrs. Peevy's office once again, Jennie asked about the Averys.

"Dana's divorced," Gladys Peevy answered willingly. "Lucy's his only daughter. He has a boy about ten. Lucy's got to be . . ." Gladys screwed up her eyes in a way that made Jennie wish she were driving instead. "Let me see, Lucy's sixteen now. Just going into her senior year at a private school over in western Connecticut. She's just gotten home for the summer, same as little Danny, who goes to school not too far from here."

"The mother didn't want the children?" Jennie asked, realizing that she might sound nosy, but feeling curious despite herself.

"Eleanor?" Gladys snorted. "Good grief, no! She took off for parts unknown. She wasn't the maternal type. It's a wonder she ever had two kids in the first place, or that she lasted here as long as she did."

"She wasn't from around here, then?"

"No. Dana met her in Boston when he was in college at Harvard. Eleanor was there, too." Gladys sighed. "They were a beautiful couple in the beginning, though—I can tell you that. She was a platinum blond—natural, too. And of course you saw for yourself how handsome Dana is." Gladys shook her head wonderingly and sighed again. "Oh, my, yes! What a couple they made at first."

"At first . . . but not later?" Jennie persisted with her questions, not knowing why.

"That's right. Later, Eleanor got to hate Stockton. 'One-horse town,' she called it. She took to drinking a little too much and started taking trips up to Boston on the spur of the moment. She lasted here a good twelve years. Everyone thought she'd never make five."

"So the little boy—Danny?—he was about five when she left?"

Gladys pursed her lips. "Six, he'd have been. Just going into first grade, he was. Cutest little boy you'd ever want to see."

Jennie let the information sink in. She didn't know why she was so interested. Hadn't she already told herself that she didn't want to get involved with Dana Avery? Then she thought about how lonely she'd been this past year. What did it matter if Dana Avery were out of the same mold as all the other men in her life? She had given up on the hope of meeting the man of her dreams. If the truth were told, she didn't even know what the man of her dreams was—she just knew that all the safe, secure, and stable men she'd dated all her life hadn't lit any sparks in her life. But maybe, at thirty-two, she was beyond having sparks lit. Maybe she should just accept that life wasn't like the books she read. Maybe she should just resign herself to security and stability and let the longed-for fireworks be damned. . . .

# Chapter Two

❧

Jennie drove slowly along the winding road, savoring the sounds and smells of the country. She had stopped at the schoolhouse for a while, wandering the property contentedly, envisioning it as it would be when the land was cleaned up and the grass mowed, when flowers had been planted and the sagging wooden steps replaced by brick ones. Now she was on her way to Grady O'Hara's place. Mrs. Peevy had given her directions, after calling him to confirm an appointment for two o'clock that afternoon.

Rounding a curve, Jennie saw the red clapboard salt-box house ahead, set behind a low stone wall and shaded by maples and oaks. A perennial border followed the gray stone wall along the side of the property, almost out of sight. Bright masses of bearded and Japanese irises, poppies, lilies, and lupines blended into one another. No mere gardener had planned this perennial border—an artist had created it. It was a living painting with colors massed together in astonishing combinations that showed unusual creativity and a sure eye.

Pulling to a stop, Jennie got out of the car and approached the front door. Nothing stirred. The quiet seemed absolute until Jennie realized that she just hadn't been listening. Pausing on the flagstone path to the pedimented front door, she realized that the leaves shifted gently overhead, riffling like pages in a book. Birds were calling to each other, hopping and darting joyously from branch to branch, crickets were chirping, and somewhere far off behind the house there was the dimly recognizable sound of a man's whistle, followed by the answering bark of a dog.

Her tap on the front door was answered almost immediately by a stern-faced woman with iron-gray hair.

"Hello. I'm Jennie Winters. I have a two-o'clock appointment with Mr. O'Hara." Jennie smiled pleasantly. "Are you Mrs. O'Hara?"

The woman's face fell so fast that Jennie was afraid it would end up on the floor. "I'm Mr. O'Hara's part-time housekeeper," the woman said, looking at Jennie as if she were from Mars. "He told me to tell you he's out back, swimming in the pond. Said to send you down there."

Jennie stood there, not knowing how to respond. Hadn't she set up an appointment for two? Why in God's name was the man *swimming* when he had agreed to meet with her? Then she remembered—Grady O'Hara was his own man. Difficult. . . .

"You just walk around the side of the house," the older woman was saying. "And follow the path down through the trees. It's quite a walk, but you'll eventually come to the pond. You can't miss it. Grady'll be there with that cussed old dog of his. Don't worry, he'll bark like hell but he won't bite. He'll be too damned afraid *you'll* bite him!" She snorted in contempt. "I told Grady the day he brought that animal home that he wasn't any good as a watchdog. Cowering all over the place, his tail between his legs . . ."

"The dog?" Jennie asked, eyes gleaming. "Or Grady?"

The woman's stern face relaxed a bit. A spark of humor gleamed momentarily in her gray eyes, then went out. "The dog," she said darkly. "Grady don't cower before man nor beast."

Jennie smiled and nodded as she backed away. "Okay, I'll remember that. Thanks for the directions."

The woman stood in the doorway and wiped her hands on her apron, her eyes openly assessing Jennie up and down. "Just follow the path," she said again, as if what she saw made her think that Jennie might get lost. "Like I say, you can't miss the pond."

Jennie picked her way carefully through the over-grown grass that began at the edge of the clipped lawn. There was a path here, but it wasn't the best she'd ever been on. Her high-heeled sandals caught on a vine and she tripped, sending her hair cascading over one shoulder. Catching her balance, Jennie swung her hair angrily back over her shoulder and walked more slowly. Lilac bushes, forsythia, rhododendron, and mountain laurel grew in a massive tangle on both sides of the path. The mountain laurel were blooming, their delicate pink blossoms almost obscuring the rich green leaves of the state flower. Overhead the sun was a golden presence in the vivid blue sky. It was unusually warm for early June. Perhaps this Grady character knew what he was doing, after all. A swim right about now would feel really good.

The path went on and on, and Jennie began to get worried. She was a city girl, used to living in a Hartford suburb. She didn't know if she liked wandering through the woods alone, sent to meet a man who supposedly cowered before neither man nor beast.

Then, just as she was about to give up and turn around, she came to a clearing. In front of her, a pond slept under the hot sun, its mirror surface broken only by a man's body slicing through the clear blue water. Jennie walked toward it, her eyes on the man. With the sun glaring off the water, she couldn't make out much about him except that he was a powerful swimmer.

His muscular arms slashed the water with ease and natural grace. His head lifted as he took a breath, and the sun caught his dark black hair, glinting on it like light on satin. Then, as quickly as it had risen, his head disappeared into the water again as he continued his powerful strokes across the water.

Jennie stood and watched, mesmerized by the graceful movement of his body. A sudden noise behind her made her stiffen, and, whirling around, she encountered the most vicious-looking dog she'd ever seen in her life. His mammoth teeth were bared in a ferocious snarl, guttural growls gurgled in his throat, and hatred seemed to dance in his eyes. As if aware of her fright, the dog put his head back and began barking savagely.

Thoroughly frightened, Jennie began to back away from the dog, one hand on her throat. She was startled into a standstill by the whiplash of a man's voice slicing through the air. "Kaiser! No!"

The barking immediately stopped and the dog changed before her eyes. He went from snarling killer to a bounding puppy with his tongue lolling out sideways from his great mouth as he ran eagerly toward her.

"No, puppy," Jennie said nervously, holding out her

hands to ward off the massive paws that were heading toward her. "No, Kaiser. Sit. Sit, Kaiser."

The dog skidded to a stop just in front of her and sat, looking up at her with friendly brown eyes, panting happily, as if this had all been one great big joke. Jennie smiled and held out a tentative hand. "Good dog. Good Kaiser."

As she let her hand trail across the soft fur on the dog's head, a man's voice spoke behind her. "You must be Ms. Winters. I'm sorry if Kaiser frightened you. He's all bark and no bite."

"So your housekeeper told me," Jennie said amicably as she began to turn around, "but I didn't . . ." Her words trailed off and she found herself staring at Grady O'Hara. He stood waist-deep in the pond and his jet-black hair was slicked back on his head, shining in the sun. His deeply tanned and muscular torso tapered into a slim waist, and his hair-sprinkled chest rose and fell with the relaxed exertion that comes after a good workout.

Jennie pulled her eyes from his body and saw that he had startling blue eyes, a square jaw, firm lips, and a slightly crooked nose. He was smiling slightly, as if amused by something he saw. But what that could be, she couldn't begin to imagine, for he was looking directly at her. . . .

Jennie was trying to get a hold on the crazy impulses that were shaking her, when he began to walk out of the water. Unwillingly her eyes traveled down the lean body, then widened in shock.

For the first time in what could have been twenty years, Jennie Winters found herself at a complete loss for words. She was thoroughly shaken as she felt an unfamiliar blush creep up her neck into her creamy-complexioned face.

"Oh," she said faintly, "you don't have any clothes on . . ." Her eyes were fastened on his body and she knew she should look away, but for some reason she couldn't. Her eyes seemed to have a will of their own, staring at the sinewed strength that stood before her. Catching her breath, she dragged her eyes away and upward, only to find him grinning at her.

"That's right," he said softly. "Stark, buck naked." He appeared completely at ease, standing knee-deep in the water, fully exposed to her sight. He pointed toward her feet. "Would you mind handing me my clothes?" he asked, smiling easily. "Or would you rather cower in the bushes while I come out and dress?"

Jennie's eyes followed the direction of his finger and fell on a pile of discarded denim. She stared at it dumbly, wondering why she hadn't noticed it before, then bent to pick it up. There were exactly three pieces of clothing—a faded pair of blue jeans, a well-worn denim shirt, and a small, navy-blue pair of bikini shorts, the kind advertised by a famous baseball player. She had often admired the baseball player in the ads she saw, but she never imagined she'd ever get quite so uncomfortably close to the product he advertised.

Straightening, she walked toward the pond. At the same time, Grady O'Hara walked out of the water. She came to an abrupt stop and waited for him, acutely aware of the hair that sprinkled his chest—dark, wiry hairs that invited caressing. . . .

Immediately she looked away—anywhere, so long as she didn't think about caressing his chest. To her acute embarrassment, she found herself staring at his lower body. Crimson color flooded her face. She snapped her eyes upward and found herself looking into the most quietly amused, startling blue eyes she had ever seen in her life.

"Did you like what you saw?" he asked softly.

She stared at him, dazed. "What?" she asked, unable to believe she had heard him correctly.

"I said, did you like what you saw?"

She moistened her lips and continued looking into those incredible blue eyes. She *had* heard him correctly. . . .

"Um . . ." She backed away and bumped against a warm wall of fur. Her surprise gave way to consternation when Kaiser began yelping, carrying on as if she were killing him. Catapulted into action, Jennie realized too late that she had backed into Kaiser and stepped on his paw with her high-heeled sandal.

"Oh!" She whirled around and reached for the dog, crooning over him. "I'm sorry, Kaiser!" she said, feeling like a complete fool. "I'm sorry, old boy." Her eyes skittered to Grady O'Hara and away again. Sure that the dog was all right, she straightened and turned her back on Grady. "All right, you can get dressed now," she said unevenly.

Jennie knew he was grinning because she could feel it burning into her back. She stood stiffly, her arms folded protectively in front of her, and squeezed her eyes shut in an effort to regain her normal composure. This was so unlike her, she didn't know what was happening. She had seen naked men before! She wasn't a child, after all. What was *wrong* with her?

"It's safe to turn around now, Ms. Winters," Grady O'Hara said from behind her.

She turned around slowly and saw that he had put on his jeans. He wore them slung low on his lean hips, in a way that emphasized the natural beauty of his body. There wasn't an ounce of superfluous flesh on him.

Jennie took a steadying breath and smiled uncertainly. "You gave me quite a shock, Mr. O'Hara. I'm afraid I'm not used to a rendezvous in the woods. . . ."

"Is that what this is?" he asked, grinning at her. "If I'd known, I'd have left my clothes off and invited you in the pond." His grin widened at the look on her face. "The water's fine," he said softly. "Just a little cold in the beginning."

She was beginning to regain her composure, but Jennie still felt off balance. This was a man so totally unlike any she had ever met that she wasn't sure how to respond to him. She had, over the years, gotten quite adept at the cocktail-party type of flirting—sexy innuendos over drinks and *hors d'oeuvres*—but this was something new in her life. Had Jane felt like this when she met Tarzan?

"Do you meet *all* your prospective clients in the buff, Mr. O'Hara?" she asked coolly. "Or just the female ones?"

A slow grin appeared on his tanned face, emphasizing the tiny webs of laugh lines that fanned out from his eyes. "I thought I'd have time for a swim before you showed up, Ms. Winters. You're the first woman in my experience who's arrived for an appointment on time."

"You must have very few female clients, then," she snapped, "because in *my* experience women are just as punctual as men, if not more so."

He bent down to retrieve a towel that was thrown carelessly on the ground and began to dry his hair. "We seem to have started out on the wrong note, Ms. Winters," he said, now toweling dry his chest and shoulders. His eyes locked with hers for a few seconds. Then he went on, filling the pregnant silence with his next words: "Why don't we start over?" He threw the towel down and walked toward her, his right hand extended. "I'm Grady O'Hara. Pleased to meet you."

She stood and stared at his outstretched hand, then took it reluctantly, feeling the heat of his hand course up her arm like an electric shock. "The pleasure, I'm afraid, has been all mine," she said wryly.

That grin appeared again, and it was even more potent up close. "Maybe I should ask for equal time, then," he said softly, "and ask you to strip so I can see what you look like."

"The only structure I want you to examine is that old schoolhouse down the road, Mr. O'Hara," she said crisply. "I'm not interested in your opinion of the soundness or structural qualities of my body."

"Pity," he said smoothly, his eyes gleaming at her. "I've a notion you'd be infinitely more fun to examine than the schoolhouse."

Jennie felt her mouth compress in a firm line. "I was told, Mr. O'Hara, that you're a competent *carpenter*. My informants seem to have left out that you're the village lothario."

A low chuckle rumbled up from his muscular chest. "I'm no lothario, Ms. Winters—just a red-blooded male who recognizes a good-looking female when he sees one." He paused, his head tipped to one side as he studied her with slightly narrowed eyes. "But you're here for business, not pleasure, I take it. Come on, let's walk over to the schoolhouse."

"Walk?" Jennie remembered the mile or more drive from the schoolhouse to here. In her high-heeled sandals, she knew she wouldn't make it all that way.

"It's only a little ways beyond the pond," Grady said, pointing toward the path that skirted the water and disappeared into a thicket on the other side.

"But . . ." Jennie frowned in bewilderment. "But I drove almost a mile to get here."

"That was taking the road, Ms. Winters," he explained patiently. "This is going through the woods, which cuts off a considerable distance. My property backs up to the schoolhouse property." He flashed a devilish smile at her. "Rather convenient, isn't it?"

Unwittingly her eyes went to her shoes and she stood biting at her lower lip, feeling indecisive. She had had enough trouble negotiating the path from his house to the pond; what would it be like going deeper into the woods?

"Oh, I see," Grady said, nodding. "You're concerned about those ridiculous shoes you're wearing." His eyes gleamed at her. "High time, too. You women don't seem to realize that they throw your posture out of alignment and can cause severe back problems—not to mention that they make you stumble all over the place so you look like a drunk on a Saturday night."

She crossed her arms and glared at him. "My shoes, Mr. O'Hara, are hardly your concern. Kindly resist making any further comments or I'll be forced to find someone else to look at the property with me."

"Ah, but who could you get who cared enough about your posture to warn you against wearing ridiculous shoes?"

She closed her eyes a moment and told herself to

count to ten, but she didn't feel like counting. Opening her eyes, she decided to favor him with a particularly frosty look.

"Mr. O'Hara."

"Yes, Ms. Winters?"

"Please shut up."

He grinned at her. "Yes, Ms. Winters."

She took a deep breath, satisfied that she had matters under control, and began to follow the path circling the pond. Her heel caught almost immediately in a tangle of grass and she began to fall. She was rescued by a pair of strong arms that came from behind and swooped her up. Before she knew what was happening, Jennie was off the ground and nestling against a warm, hair-covered chest, strong arms cradling her as audacious blue eyes laughed into hers.

"Perhaps I should carry you," he said softly.

She felt alarming sensations shaking her. Under her hands, Grady's skin was warm and firm and sensually exciting. There was a faint odor of dampness about him, coupled with the natural, slightly musky scent from his male body. And his lips were uncomfortably close, drawing her eyes like magnets. Unconsciously she moistened her own lips as she stared at those firm lips so close to her own.

"Um . . . I don't think so," she murmured, feeling her voice break. She cleared her throat and a quick glance at his eyes told her he was laughing at her even more. She wanted to strike him for that, but she was afraid she would fall if she let go of his strong neck. So instead of hitting him, she clung to him, all the while swamped by unfamiliar emotions and physical stirrings. "I think you better put me down," she whispered, her eyes wide.

His eyes did a slow exploration of her, moving lazily across her hair and forehead, down past her eyes to her nose and lips and staying there for a time, then moving upward to her eyes again.

"Yes," he murmured. "I think I better."

Before she knew it, her feet were on solid ground again, but the strong arms remained around her and she was still caught up against that naked, warm chest. Her hands knotted against him as her head tilted to look into his eyes.

"Have you caught your balance yet?" he asked softly.

She nodded unsteadily and pushed away from him. At the same moment, he released her. Jennie hadn't realized how close they were to the edge of the pond, and she suddenly felt herself falling. She let out a startled whoop of fear, then tumbled backward through the air. She caught only a glimpse of Grady's astonished look and his outstretched hands reaching for her before all was confusion. She was in the water, sitting on her rump, spluttering like a beached whale while the dog, Kaiser, was barking excitedly and running back and forth along the edge of the pond. On the bank, Grady O'Hara was roaring with laughter, his head thrown back on his powerful neck, his teeth gleaming white against his tan face.

Wiping the back of her hand across her mouth, Jennie glared up at him. Who did he think he was, laughing at her? He should be *helping* her, damn it, not standing up there cracking up! She pushed her soaking hair out of her eyes and struggled to her feet, but the bottom of the pond was muddy, her shoes were slick, and she went down again, choking and spluttering from the second dunking.

"Ohh, *damn!*" she wailed as she surfaced.

If it was possible, Grady O'Hara was laughing even harder, bent over and slapping his knee with pure enjoyment. Still in the water, her hair dripping around her face and shoulders like seaweed, Jennie seethed with anger. How would *he* like it if he fell in and she stood there laughing like a hyena?

Jennie saw red, and without thinking scrambled out of the water and made straight for him. Grabbing his hands, she planted her feet and tugged. He went over easily, his large body spinning past her to land with a huge splash in the water. Unfortunately, she hadn't taken time to plant herself well enough, and she followed him into the pond, dunked for the third time in less than a minute.

Kaiser went mad, barking wildly as he ran in ever-widening circles. At the noise he created, a covey of birds broke from the surrounding trees, their raucous cries and flapping wings adding even more noise to the total chaos. At the height of all the noise, Kaiser circled the pond, running at full tilt, then headed right for Jennie and Grady, who were just beginning to struggle to their feet. Grady saw Kaiser coming just as the huge dog launched himself into midair.

"Ohh, nooo—" Grady's shout was cut off by ninety pounds of frenzied dog hitting him smack in the middle of his chest. They went over with a loud splash, Kaiser ecstatic at this new game his master was playing.

Meanwhile, Jennie struggled toward the edge of the pond, her feet slipping and sliding on the muddy bottom until she was finally able to drag herself ashore. For a moment she lay panting in the long grass; then she rolled over and raised her head to survey the damage.

Kaiser was joyously pawing his master, whose curses formed a blue haze over his head. "Damn you, Kaiser," Grady roared. "*Down!*"

Kaiser obviously thought "down" meant "up," for he launched himself once again toward his master's chest, knocking Grady off balance and into the water once more.

Jennie sat up and began to giggle. It was really very funny. No *wonder* Grady had been laughing at her. And *this* was even funnier, for Kaiser was persistent in his game and Grady's curses were steadily escalating in both strength and color.

Jennie's giggles turned into outright laughter. Struggling to her feet, she pointed toward man and dog and tried to stop laughing, but it wasn't any use.

"Oh!" she whooped, losing her breath and struggling to catch it. "Oh!" She got hold of herself and straightened in time to see Grady advancing on her, a murderous look in his eyes. She fell into another spasm of laughter, bending over almost double to try to ease the pain that was gripping her stomach.

"Ohhhh!" she screamed with laughter. "You look so damn *funny!*"

"Not as funny as you're going to look," he snarled, but then he too was laughing as he gathered her into his arms and held her out over the pond.

"No!" she screamed, laughter beginning to mingle with fear. "Grady, no! Don't!"

"Do you promise to do anything I want?" he asked, holding her even farther out over the water.

Her laughter began to fade, taken over by common sense. She didn't want to get thrown in again, but she didn't know what he'd ask her to do, either. She hesitated, and she felt his muscles tense in preparation to throw her in. "Yes!" she yelled. "I promise!"

"Anything?" he asked, still poised at the edge of the pond.

She gulped, the laughter now completely gone. "Anything."

He stepped back and slowly let her down. As her feet touched the ground, she tried to push out of his arms, but he held her tightly.

"Oh, no, you don't, Ms. Winters," he murmured. His arms felt like steel cables around her. "Not so fast. We've got some unfinished business to take care of."

She put her palms against the wet, hair-roughened surface of his chest and tilted her head up, her eyes widening quizzically. "We do?" she asked.

"We do." His voice was low and slightly raspy and Jennie was suddenly aware of her own wet body plastered against his. She shivered slightly, unable to look away from those hypnotic blue eyes that held her. "You're shivering," he murmured, holding her against him so that her hips were pressed into his.

She could feel the rising bulge in his jeans and felt delicious tremors of physical longing shake her. She knew she should try to move away, to put some distance between them, but her body wouldn't respond. Defying her, it pressed against Grady even harder, causing a flame to leap in the blue furnace of his eyes.

"You need to dry off," he murmured, his breath feathering her lips. "Your clothes are all wet. You'll catch cold."

His voice was like cut glass gliding across velvet, husky and low and sensual, and it sent a tingling awareness throughout her midsection. Her breasts rose and fell as her breathing became more labored. She was unable to tear her eyes away from his, unable to stop the physical sensations that were swamping her. Her hands moved across the muscular expanse of chest, savoring the wet, warm skin.

"I'm . . ." Her voice cracked and she began again. "I'm fine," she protested, trying to push away. But his arms only strengthened their hold on her, pulling her closer and flaming the fires that were already raging in her veins. Even as she tried to shake her head in denial, Jennie's hands were sliding around the firm rib cage to his back, gliding upward to his muscular shoulders. Her head tilted back farther and her lips parted in invitation.

Grady's lips came down in slow hunger, taking hers with lazy, sensual thoroughness, nibbling, tasting, back and forth, back and forth, arousing her to a frenzy, then kissing her harder, the passion mounting as he sensed her response.

She groaned and melted against him, all resistance gone. Her hands pressed into his back in an agony of need as a warmth pulsed through her, washing over her in wave after wave of delicious sensations. Against her abdomen, the hardness of Grady O'Hara was tantalizing, beckoning her and promising all manner of delights. Her body responded, filled with aching need, and she pushed closer.

His tongue invaded her mouth, and Jennie groaned in ecstasy. Her own tongue took up the mating dance, circling his in a velvet cadence. But it wasn't enough. They broke apart, their breathing ragged as Grady's lips sought the soft, sensitive skin just under her left ear.

Jennie began to shake. This was like nothing she had ever experienced. She was on fire, tossed by a storm

and immersed in a violent sea of passion. There was no
holding back, no stopping. She was gripped by a need
so powerful that her intellect was drowned in physical
sensation.

Her breath escaped in ragged gasps against the hair-
roughened chest. Her fingers glided unceasingly up and
down the smooth back, caressing the rippling muscles as
the fires built inside her.

"Grady . . ." she whispered, and it came out as a
moan. "Please . . ."

Her breath caught in her throat as he lowered her to
the ground and pinned her there, his fingers already
beginning their slow, sure movements with the buttons
at the neck of her T-shirt. Shakily she reached down and
fastened her fingers on the zipper of his jeans and tugged
it down, then moved her hands into the damp warmth of
his jeans, molding her fingers to the muscles that bunched
beneath the back pockets of his jeans.

She heard his low chuckle against her breasts. Her
T-shirt and bra had been dragged off and flung to one
side and already his mouth was feasting on her breasts.

"You're greedy, aren't you, little one?" he murmured,
his tongue flicking over one aroused pink nipple.

Her breath shook as she inhaled the delicious scent
from his skin. "Yes," she whispered. "Very greedy."
Filled with longing, she moved her hands up his back to
his shoulders, her eyes closing as she savored the feel of
his skin and the warmth of the sun beating down on his
back and heating it under his hands. So smooth, she
thought hazily, his skin is so smooth. . . .

Then her mind went blank and she was once again
carried beyond rational thought. "Grady," she whispered shakily. "Please, touch me . . ."

A low groan escaped him as his mouth fastened on the tip of her left breast and his tongue began to flick the hardened nub back and forth in a steadily mounting rhythm.

"Grady . . ." Her hands moved unceasingly over his broad back. "Grady, please . . ."

But he was intent on letting his lips and tongue take a slow journey down her midriff. When he came to the waistband of her jeans, he paused long enough to pull the snap apart and lower the zipper. He tugged her jeans and underpants off her hips in one smooth movement, then stripped them from the long length of her legs. He knelt over her, his mouth continuing its downward journey, taking small, unplanned side trips to her hips and then nuzzling into the soft skin at the top of her thighs.

Shaking almost uncontrollably, she opened herself to him and his delicious journey came to its explosive end. Gasping, her fingers weaving into his hair, she felt as if a tidal wave were beginning to rise far offshore. She could almost see it behind her closed lids, a thin silver line on a far horizon. As Grady stood up and shucked off his clothes, it was gathering strength, growing on the far blue horizon. Then Grady lowered himself onto her, his body large and warm, enveloping Jennie completely. As he nuzzled her soft, vulnerable core, she felt the hot, liquid heat melting the substance of her body.

The sensation that a tidal wave was bearing down on her grew. Now it was a huge wave, blotting out the horizon, building and building in strength, coming ever closer, the top edge mounting to the sky, just beginning to curl over as it neared the shore.

But Grady wouldn't let it crash home. He held it off,

controlling it by his movements and managing to keep her at fever pitch, poised just at the crest. Her body moved in elemental rhythm with his, all sweet, aching beauty, at one with the universe.

And then, blotting out all thought, Grady thrust deeply and brought the wave crashing home, splintering their world into a thousand pinpoints of golden light. Submerged in it, she shouted his name.

"Grady!"

The cry shattered the quiet air, seeming to bounce off the clear blue sky that formed a canopy over them, echoing in their ears even as the thundering wave receded, leaving only silence and contentment.

Grady relaxed against her, his body warm on hers, his breathing still unsteady but slowly calming. They remained silent for a time, wrapped in a cocoon of peace. Then Grady levered himself up onto one elbow and stared down into her eyes.

"Lady," he said wonderingly, his eyes locked on hers, "I don't even know your first name."

She stared up into those blue eyes and felt her world tilt off its axis. In the space of a few minutes she had changed irrevocably and she knew nothing would ever be the same. She had shattered the mold, throwing out the past.

"It's Jennie," she whispered, staring back at him. "Jennie Winters. . . ."

# Chapter Three

As soon as Grady stood up to dress, reality overwhelmed Jennie. What had she *done*? She had just made love with a stranger five minutes after meeting him, and in the *grass*! She felt physically sick as the full impact of her actions hit her.

Oh, God, she moaned to herself, what have I done?

Reaching quickly for her underpants, she pulled them on and dived for her bra. Fumbling with the hook, she got it safely on, then stood up and reached for her jeans. Still soaked, they felt like lead weights. Gamely she put her right foot in, then stepped in with her left foot. She tried to pull the jeans up, then stopped.

Standing there, partially dressed, she realized why people never tried to put on wet blue jeans, particularly figure-molding designer jeans: when one pulled, the jeans simply didn't respond. They sat like lead around her knees, refusing to budge.

Angrily she pulled harder and was rewarded by the merest upward movement before they stopped once again, held back, she supposed, by the deadweight of the waterlogged denim. Not bothering to suppress the anger she felt, Jennie cursed and pulled again, wiggling back and forth in her effort. Slowly, with lots of tugging and much wiggling of her behind, the jeans inched upward until they finally covered her hips.

The zipper, though, still remained to be zipped. Completely exhausted by her efforts to pull up the jeans, Jennie paused for breath, stealing a glance toward Grady. What she saw sent a furious color leaping into her face. He was standing with arms folded, watching her with eyes that gleamed with amusement. His lips quivered as he fought to suppress a grin.

"What'd they do? Shrink?" His grin broke out of control. "Or does it always take that much work for you to dress?" His eyes were like explosions of blue fireworks. "You sure did look cute, though," he added softly. "I like the way you wiggle."

Jennie glared at him, and turned away, putting her back to him as she struggled with her zipper. "Just attend to your own clothing, Mr. O'Hara, and I'll attend to mine."

"But I'm already dressed," he said, his voice coming from behind her, too close for comfort. "And you look like you could use some help."

Jennie put as much distance as she could between them. "You just keep away, do you hear?" she said shrilly.

Never in all her life had she been so embarrassed. What had come *over* her? Her face flamed as she remembered her behavior. Then another hot flash of humiliation swept over her. How could she face him? What did he think of her? She died internally as the answer invaded her mind: he probably thought she jumped into bed with every willing male. . . .

Her fingers shook as she fumbled with her zipper. "Damn!" she muttered. What was *wrong* with it?

"Here. Let me help." Grady swung her around and fastened gentle fingers on hers. Jennie knew he was trying to get her to look at him, but she flatly refused, keeping her eyes firmly on the ground at her feet.

He sighed softly and began tugging on the zipper. "I think they did shrink," he said, grinning again. "Either that or you put on an awful lot of weight in the past few minutes." He paused fractionally, his grin widening. "And I doubt that that's possible, what with the workout you just had."

Jennie felt her breath catch sharply as anger and embarrassment clashed. "Must you *talk* about it?" she demanded indignantly.

"Talk about what?" Grady asked, still tugging on her zipper.

She dared to glance at him with ice-frosted eyes. He met her glance and held it. "Talk about what, Jennie Winters?" he asked softly.

She stared at him, sighed deeply, and looked away. "About *it.*"

"It? What's 'it'?"

She felt like hitting him, but contented herself with adding more ice to her eyes. If he thought she was going to stand here and make civilized conversation about her uncivilized behavior as if she were at a garden party, he had another think coming!

"Look," she said, her anger barely leashed, "I know what you must think of me—"

"You do?" he interrupted.

"But it's not true," she went on as if he hadn't spoken.

"It's not?"

She sent him a blood-chilling glance and continued her train of thought: "I don't usually . . ." She faltered, trying to find the right words to explain herself, but none came. She hit at his hands in frustration and whirled away. "Dammit! I'll zip my own zipper, thank you!"

He chuckled but appeared content to let her struggle alone. "So what do you think I think of you, Jennie Winters?"

She ignored him, swearing at the recalcitrant zipper that was slowly inching its way upward. "Do shut up!" she snapped. "Can't you see I need to *concentrate*?"

"It must take you a couple hours *every* morning to dress. I hope you live alone—if anyone *ever* tried to say good morning or read you something from the newspaper, you'd probably *never* get dressed." His eyes sparkled devilishly. "If *I* lived with you, I'd be reading to you all the time—"

"Oh, do shut up!" she snapped, the zipper finally zipped and the closure fastened. "Hand me my shirt."

Grady good-naturedly leaned down and picked up her T-shirt, then hesitated. "Uh-oh," he said, peering up at her after examining the shirt. "There's one of those little animals on your shirt."

"*What* little animal?" she shrieked. Had a frog or snake crawled into it? Thank God Grady had picked it up.

He held it out, pointing to the emblem. "This little animal."

Her eyes fell on the alligator, and the gold flecks in her eyes caught fire. Yanking the shirt from his hands and bristling at his broad grin, she jammed the shirt over her head and pulled it over her shapely breasts.

"I have a theory why women wear those shirts with those little emblems on them," Grady said.

"Do you?" Ice tinkled in the words.

"Yep, I do." He grinned at her amiably. "My theory is that those designers are smart. They know without ever coming right out and *saying* it that a woman buys her clothes to attract men."

He had her attention despite herself. "Do they?"

"Mmm hmm. They do." He laid his index finger lightly on the emblem. "See where they put that alligator?" He glanced up at her, his eyes gleaming. "Catches a man's eye every time. Women know men are going to look at their breasts when they have on this kind of shirts."

Furious that she had even listened to his ridiculous theory, Jennie yanked the ribbon from her hair. "It's a novel theory," she said, twisting the excess water from her hair and putting the ribbon back in it. "But I don't buy it."

He shrugged. "Well, like I say, it's only a theory. I haven't done any empirical tests on it or anything."

Jennie flashed an astonished glance at him. For some reason, he didn't quite fit the usual stereotype of the local carpenter. . . . Then everything that had happened between them came flooding back to her and she put a hand to her head. She had a headache coming on. If only there were a way to wipe out the past half hour.

"Look. Mr. O'Hara—"

"Why so formal? You called me Grady when we were making love."

Jennie closed her eyes briefly and took a deep breath. She couldn't face him. Crossing her arms, she looked out over the pond, her face unmoving. "Look . . . *Grady*. Perhaps it would be best if I found another carpenter."

"You won't find one better than me."

"I'm sure that's true. You were highly recommended. All the same, under the circumstances, I think it's best if—"

"What circumstances?" Grady interrupted.

Jennie let out a breath. A headache was definitely on its way. She kneaded her forehead and wished she could quietly sink to the bottom of the pond and die. "The *present* circumstances," she answered carefully.

"I'm afraid I don't understand." He was grinning again. That awful man was *grinning* again! If she had a weapon, she'd swing it and permanently put his gleaming white teeth out of commission.

She steeled herself to continue. "Mr. O'Hara—"

"Grady."

"Grady. Despite what you think, this is *not* my normal behavior."

"Nor mine, Ms. Winters."

She flicked him a surprised glance, then looked away quickly. "And under the circumstances—"

"*What* circumstances?" he repeated. "You keep saying that, but I'm not sure what you mean."

She took a deep breath and let it out slowly. He really was the most annoying man. "Mr. O'Hara . . . Grady . . ." She paused, unable to think of how to say it. How did a woman explain behavior such as hers? It was inexcusable. Absolutely unpardonable. "Dammit," she exploded, "I don't just go around screwing every man in sight, you know!"

He wiped his hand across his mouth but was unable to completely hide the smile that hovered on his lips. "I'm sure you don't, Ms. Winters . . . Jennie."

She glared at him. "Then wipe that damn smile off your face!"

He cleared his throat and twisted his neck uncomfortably, but his deep laughter burst out despite any attempts to stop it. "Look, Jennie—"

"Don't you Jennie me!" she cried, shaking with anger.

"Look . . ." His voice was gentle but still clearly amused. "Calm down, okay? It was only a . . ." He saw the murderous look enter her eyes and his words trailed off. "Um . . ." He seemed to be scouting around for the best way to say it; then his eyes softened and he shook his head slowly back and forth. "Hey," he said softly. "It's okay. Honest. It was nice."

Something in his tone, or perhaps it was the gentle warmth in his eyes, reached her. She felt herself begin to relax, and the awkward situation suddenly didn't seem as horrible as it had. She looked down at the ground and saw her bare toes curling into the grass. "I . . . I've never done anything like that before," she said. "I feel funny."

He fastened his large hand on her chin and gently tilted her head up so she had to meet his gaze. His thumb moved caressingly on her cheek as he studied her. "Don't," he murmured. "You'll ruin it. And it was too nice to ruin."

She stared into his eyes, uncertain of how to react. This was so incredibly different from anything that had ever happened to her that she felt completely at a loss for words. She let out a breath and smiled wryly. "Yeah," she muttered. "Well . . ."

He grinned at her. "That's better."

She grinned back, still feeling strange yet also feeling oddly comfortable with him. It was almost as if they'd known each other for a long time and needed no facades and games. But that thought made her so frightened that she pulled away. "Well, I guess I better go. . . ." She felt as awkward as a schoolgirl, not knowing where to put her hands. She finally stuffed them into her jeans pockets, only to realize there wasn't much room in her jeans pockets. She took them out and made a vague gesture toward his house. "I'll just go get my car."

"I thought we were going to walk over to the schoolhouse."

She stopped suddenly. "Well, I . . ." *Now* what did she do? She obviously couldn't ask the man to *work* for her. It would be impossible! Surely he didn't think she still wanted him to look at the schoolhouse, much less do any of the work? "Well," she said, hedging carefully, "you see, I've reconsidered."

"About buying the schoolhouse?"

"Er . . . no, not about the *schoolhouse*."

"What about, then?" he gently goaded her, urging her to speak.

"About *you*."

"What about me?"

She rolled her eyes and turned her back on him in exasperation. "Good grief, Grady O'Hara! You can't expect me to hire you *now*!"

"Why not?"

His voice was so calm and matter-of-fact that she whirled around to face him. "Why *not?*" she cried. "After what *happened?*"

His eyes glittered warmly, still looking amused. "I don't see what that's got to do with anything. I'm still just as good a carpenter now as I was before I made love to you."

She closed her eyes and put her hand to her head. Where was his *tact?* Did he have to say it right out in the *open* like that? "Oh, God," she moaned. "I have a terrible headache."

"You've got it backward, darlin'," he drawled. "You're supposed to say that *before*, not after."

"Would that I had," she moaned softly, then felt a wet tongue licking her hand. Looking down, she met Kaiser's brown eyes and suddenly her sense of humor began to surface. "Don't *you* start in on me too," she said, stroking the dog's velvety head.

"Why not?" Grady asked. "He's my dog. He's going to help all he can."

She turned her head to look at Grady, and suddenly his eyes were serious. The laughter had died out. She stood and gazed at him, finally making her decision.

"Okay," she said. "I'd like you to at least look at the schoolhouse with me, but . . ."

"But?"

She hesitated, gnawing at her lip. "If . . . if I were to hire you . . ."

"Yes," he prompted gently. "If you were to hire me . . ."

"It'd be strictly business. No more funny business."

"Is that what it was by the pond, Jennie Winters?" he asked softly. "Funny business?"

She reacted to his voice with a slight shiver; its tone brought back the sensual memories. Rubbing her arms to chase away the goose bumps, she met his eyes coolly. "Is that clear, Mr. O'Hara? This could never happen again. *Never.*"

"What are you afraid of, Jennie?" he asked, his voice low and intimate.

"I'm not afraid of anything!" she cried, then took a conscious breath to calm herself. "I'm not afraid of anything," she repeated quietly. "I just want our relationship to be clear."

He studied her a moment, then shrugged, his hands stuck in his back pants pockets. "Okay by me," he said, grinning amiably. "You're the boss."

She hesitated, peering at him cautiously, then nodded. "Okay, but that has to be clear. I *am* the boss, and you'll work for me. Nothing more."

He shrugged again, pulling her eyes momentarily to the muscles in his arms. "Whatever you say, it's okay by me."

Catching herself before she could react to his body, Jennie leaned down and slipped on her shoes. "Okay, then lead me to this so-called path of yours. And walk slowly, please. These jeans feel like they're drying into cement."

Grady grinned lopsidely as his eyes swept over her assessingly, but he refrained from comment. He leaned down and picked up his shirt and shrugged into it, buttoning it halfway up; then he started down the path.

Startled by the pang of regret she felt at his quick acquiescence, Jennie followed him. It would be all right, she told herself. They were adults. They could work together and not be involved personally.

But as her eyes studied the man walking in front of her, Jennie felt a dizzying rush of physical desire begin to churn in her stomach. Suddenly she wasn't so sure. Maybe he could work for her, but could she stand to be around him without repeating this afternoon's incredible lovemaking?

# Chapter Four

❧

"Do you want to restore or just remodel?" Grady called back over his shoulder to Jennie.

Jennie muttered a low curse at a branch that had just missed her cheek as she plunged through the overgrown path. Grady's broad-shouldered back was up ahead, just within sight.

"What?" she called, stopping to catch her breath. "I can't hear you."

Grady turned around and grinned. When she finally caught up with him, he repeated himself. "I asked if you wanted to restore the schoolhouse or just remodel it."

Jennie brushed her damp, straggling hair back from her eyes. "What's the difference?" she asked. "I just want to live in the place." She heaved a sigh and cast Grady a disparaging look. "I thought you said the schoolhouse was close by. I feel like I'm on a ten-mile hike."

"It's up ahead, just around the next bend. We're almost there."

Jennie nodded, then made a face as she shook one leg, then the other. Her jeans were clinging to her legs like vines of ivy. If she didn't keep moving, it was possible she'd be stuck out in these woods for life. Grady would either have to chop them off her or call for help from the volunteer fire department. She glanced at him and saw that he was grinning at her. Irritated, Jennie pushed past him and doggedly marched forward.

"So what's the difference between restoration and renovation?" she asked. "They sound the same to me."

Grady materialized at her side. "There's a big difference," he said. "A lot depends on how you want to live. Some people see an old place and want to restore it exactly as it was when it was built. That's called historic restoration. That might entail using wooden pegs instead of nails and scouring the countryside for the right kind of hardware for the cabinets and doors. Some people are such purists that they even restore the kitchen as authentically as possible, cooking their meals in a beehive brick oven and pumping their water by hand."

Jennie made a face. "You're kidding!"

Grady laughed, but shook his head. "They end up living in a historically accurate building, but it's almost like living in a museum.

"Then there are other people who want to restore the place to *look* historically accurate but they don't want to worry about using pegs instead of nails and that sort of thing. These are the people who want modern, up-to-date kitchens and baths. They're not interested in living in a museum, but they do want the charm of an older building. This is sometimes called interpretive restoration—it's striving for functional living in building that's as authentic as possible."

"That sounds more like it," Jennie said under her breath.

Grady caught her words and his grin widened into a

smile. "Then there are others who just like the looks of an old place and want to keep its inherent charm but they want it completely gutted and modernized."

Jennie glanced at Grady, nodding as she picked her way carefully through the tall weeds and grass. He had warmed to his subject and his face was animated, his eyes glowing as he looked down at her. "Often," he continued, "you'll see an old factory or brownstone redone this way. The brick walls might be kept, but skylights and huge modern windows are added. Attics might be taken out and the ceiling removed to expose the rafters for cathedral ceilings—that sort of thing." He smiled at the look on Jennie's face. "What's the matter? Are you chickening out already?"

Jennie raised an eyebrow. "I just want it to be comfortable and easy to take care of. It's going to be a weekend home, a place to get away to. I don't want to have to hire a *curator* for the damn thing!"

Grady's rich laugh warmed the air around them. "Well, if it's comfort and ease of upkeep you want, I'd recommend either a complete modernization or a combination approach. You could restore the outside to be historically accurate but gut the inside and add a modern kitchen and bath. You could make it as efficient as possible, but still retain the essential warmth and charm of the original woodwork and flooring and any other architectural details we find."

Jennie nodded. "And how expensive is that?" She realized she had to start getting practical. It was fine to dream about a new weekend home, but she also had to pay for it.

"This way isn't as expensive as a full historic restoration," he answered. "That's where the big money comes

in, mostly because of the painstaking work that has to
be done by the restorer. If you just fix up the outside
and redo the interior, it won't be as expensive.''

"But how much?" she persisted.

He grinned a slow, easy grin and reached out to snap
a twig off a branch. Chewing on it lazily, he smiled into
her eyes. "That's what we're here to find out. Don't go
jumping the gun on me, Jennie Winters. You're going to
need a septic tank and plumbing and electricity. Those
all take time and a fair amount of money, not to mention all the appliances, the masonry work for a chimney,
a heating system—''

"But how *much?*" Jennie asked stubbornly. She was
beginning to wonder if Grady O'Hara ever answered a
question with a simple response.

He sighed and scratched his chin thoughtfully, the
twig still clamped between his strong teeth. "Well, let's
see . . . three to five thousand for the plumbing, electricity,
and septic system. You've got a well, but you'll need a
pump, so that's another few hundred. You'll need a
heating system if you plan to use the place year round
. . ." He shrugged. "I'll have to do a detailed inspection
to see if there are any structural problems that would add
to the expenses." He looked down at her and grinned
around the twig. "I guess I'm saying it's too early to tell.
It could be twelve thousand, it could be twenty, maybe
even twenty-five.''

Jennie digested that, adding the figures to the cost of
the property and beginning to wonder if she knew what
she was getting into. She looked up at him. "Is there a
way to cut corners and save a few thousand here and
there?''

"There are always ways to save on a construction

project. The first thing you have to remember is that all you really have to do to make the schoolhouse habitable is to put in electricity, plumbing, and heating. Any cosmetic changes can be put off for as long as you want. And one sure way to cut costs is to do some of the work yourself."

Jennie stared at him. "Oh." She wondered what that might entail. "What kind of work?"

"Well . . ." He shrugged easily, drawing her eyes to his well-built shoulders and muscled arms. She was so engrossed in looking at him that she almost missed what he had to say. "I usually hire an assistant," he was saying, "but you could fill in."

Jennie felt her ears prick up. There was no need to try to concentrate now—he had her undivided attention. "You mean . . .?"

"That's right," he said, grinning at the look on her face. "You could be my assistant. That'd just mean holding boards for me when I nailed them, handing me tools, that sort of thing. Nothing strenuous or particularly difficult. You could also do a lot of the stripping . . ." At the threatening look that crossed Jennie's face, he laughed.

"Stripping paint," he said gently. "Off doors and woodwork."

Thoroughly chastened for jumping to the wrong conclusion, Jennie felt her face grow red. She tossed her still-damp hair haughtily and glared at him. "Oh. *That* kind of stripping."

Grady's eyes bounced off hers. He looked down at the ground and tried to suppress a wide grin, but he wasn't very successful. "Yes," he said softly. "That kind." He took a deep breath and went on. "You could also do finish painting and perhaps tape the wallboard. You might even want to redo the floors yourself. That can be a messy job, but some women are really good at it." He glanced back at her. "So you see, there are all kinds of things you could do, and save money at the same time."

Jennie found herself intrigued by the idea of doing part of the work herself, of contributing toward turning the old schoolhouse into a warm, livable home. Equally intriguing was the idea of working alongside Grady O'Hara, though as soon as she admitted it, she pushed the thought aside.

"I couldn't work during the week," she cautioned. "I have a job."

"Well, then, on weekends," Grady suggested. "I have a couple of jobs that are winding down right now, so I'd be ready to start work on a new project in a few weeks. I'd be willing to work with you on weekends, and I'd probably be able to manage a day or two during the week to be here while the subcontractors come in to work."

"Subcontractors?"

"The plumber, electrician, mason—I'd do the actual carpentry work and act as general contractor and supervisor, but I'd hire out the various specialty jobs."

"I see." It all sounded much more complicated than Jennie had imagined when she first saw the schoolhouse. "I'll have to get another couple of contractors to look the place over, of course," she said. "I mean, I'll want to have at least two or three competitive bids," she added stiffly. "I'm not promising you the job, Mr. O'Hara."

His blue eyes glittered with humor. "Of course, Ms. Winters. I understand."

His answering formality mocked hers, making her acutely conscious of what had gone on between them only a half-hour before. She had the distinct feeling that he was remembering as well. The unspoken knowledge of their shared intimacy at the pond seemed to heat the air around them. It was as if an invisible cord linked them. To the world, they were strangers, and only they knew what had happened between them.

Grady's matter-of-fact voice interrupted her thoughts. "Here we are," he said smoothly, leading her out of the woods into a clearing. He stopped and gazed at the back of the schoolhouse, suddenly all business as he inspected it. "It's a beautiful old building," he said. "I'm glad somebody has finally seen its potential."

Jennie glanced at him with interest. "Do you work solely with old buildings?"

"That's right. I guess you could say they're my passion. I love their strength, their history, their aura. They were built with love by craftsmen." His lips curved into a smile as he gazed at the schoolhouse. "They're worth preserving, they keep us in touch with our roots."

Jennie felt oddly warmed by his words. It was obvious he spoke with a quiet but deeply held conviction. That touched her. Many of her acquaintances held no firm beliefs, had no anchors in this fast-paced world. If anything, they were all searching for something to believe in. Grady O'Hara seemed to have found whatever he had searched for and Jennie found that comforting. She turned her eyes toward the schoolhouse and wondered if that was what had drawn her to it in the first place—the swift, intuitive knowledge that here she would find something to believe in, somewhere to put down roots.

But she wondered if he would approve of her desire

to modernize the interior. Was he one of those purists he had mentioned? "How do you feel about my wanting to gut the interior and make it modern?" she asked, trying to sound casual, not wanting him to know how much his approval mattered. She didn't even understand it herself. What did it matter if he approved? He was just a carpenter. . . .

Grady smiled down at her. "This is just a one-room country schoolhouse, Jennie. It's not historically or even architecturally important. If it were, then I'd be all for doing a full and accurate historical restoration. It *is* a wonderful old building, though, filled with the warmth and character of a lost era. It deserves to be fixed up and lived in. You seem to want to do that and I'm all for helping someone who wants to preserve a part of our past." He grinned at her. "Does that answer your question?"

She grinned back, warmed by his response. "Yes, sir, it does."

"Good." He drew a small leather pouch from his back pocket and started walking toward the schoolhouse. "Then let's get started. I'll do a preliminary inspection for structural integrity, then we can talk about what you might want to do both inside and out. I'll be able to give you an estimate, but it'll be only a rough one. After you get estimates from a couple of other contractors, you can decide whether or not you want to hire me. If you do, we'll go over this place with a fine-tooth comb and I'll give you a detailed bid in writing, complete with estimated starting and completion dates."

He approached the building with slow steps, looking around at the surroundings. "One of the first things you should think about when you're considering buying an old place is the surroundings." He looked at her briefly and smiled warmly. "As you can see, you couldn't find a better location. I own most of the land to the right and don't plan to build on it, so it'll stay quiet and rural. Dana Avery owns the land off to the left and I know he's not planning to build on it. He leases the hayfields to an old cuss who'll still be haying when he's ninety-nine."

Jennie found herself grinning with Grady, her eyes shining as she looked at the property from this new perspective.

He pointed to the sky. "The back of the schoolhouse faces south. That's important—you'll get solar warming in the winter on that side. Since the back is away from the road and out of sight, you might want to consider adding a greenhouse or sunroom off a kitchen area." He paused and looked at the maples and oaks that threw heavy shade. "In the winter, these deciduous trees will shed their leaves and the sun will warm the place all day. I'd recommend you combine a greenhouse with solar heating, and use a wood stove for backup heating."

Jennie stared at the schoolhouse, envisioning a greenhouse where the dilapidated wooden stoop now stood. She felt her excitement rising. What fun to go hunting for wicker furniture and turn the greenhouse addition into a year-round tropical paradise with flowers and plants growing in profusion amid colorfully cushioned furniture.

Grady walked slowly around the building, his eyes moving steadily, missing nothing. He inspected the roof visually, then let his eyes travel down the paint-chipped clapboards to the masonry foundation. Stooping, he prodded the masonry, then stood up and continued his appraisal. Occasionally he would kneel to get a closer look at the foundation. Jennie knelt alongside him, her amber-flecked eyes glowing with excitement.

"What are you looking for?" she asked, feeling like a child on Christmas morning.

"I'm looking for cracks," he said absently. "And trying to see if there are signs of water leaking into the basement."

"Are there?"

"Can't see any," he said. "There's a good slope away from the foundation, so water should drain away from the building. We'll be able to tell better when we look at the basement."

He stood up and peered at the window frames. Jennie clasped her hands behind her back and followed suit. "How do they look?" she asked.

He grinned at her. "Not bad. No signs of rotting wood. Of course, the paint has chipped away badly, so it'll have to be scraped down and redone." His blue eyes gleamed at her. "That'd be a good job for you."

She looked back at the window frame and saw it with new eyes. There was a certain amount of pride mixed in with skepticism at the thought that she could scrape down old, peeling paint and then redo the windows. "Is it hard?" she asked.

"Nope," he said easily. "Donkey work."

She glanced at him, saw that he was teasing, and relaxed. "I suppose that means you have to be an ass to get stuck doing it."

He laughed easily. "You said it, not me."

They fell into a companionable silence as he did a slow, thorough tour around the rest of the building. When they had gone full circle, Grady came to a stop and rubbed his chin. He had long ago discarded the twig he had been chewing on. "Roof looks good from here. I'll have to do a closer inspection, of course, but there aren't any loose shingles that I can see. If I remember correctly, Dana reroofed this place about five years ago. That means it could last you another twenty years or so. The chimney's in rough shape, though, so I'd recommend having a mason rebuild it. These older ones usually weren't lined, and you'll need that if you put in a wood stove. The window and door frames are square and sturdy, and overall the building looks sound on the outside." He glanced at her and smiled that beguiling smile of his. "Now, if you've got the key, we can go inside and check it out. That will tell us the real story."

Jennie remembered that she had slipped the key into her jeans pocket. She drew in her breath and slid her slim hand into the right pocket, wiggling her fingers deeper and deeper into the tight space. She finally felt the key and grasped it with her fingertips to pull it out.

"Whew," she said, "for a while I thought I wouldn't be able to get it."

"It could always be surgically removed," Grady drawled lazily and took the key from her hand.

For a second his strong fingers came into contact with hers and she felt an electric pulse travel through her. Looking up, she saw he was watching her quietly, as if upon touching her he too had experienced the sudden shock of physical awareness. She looked away quickly, not wanting to prolong the moment. During their tour of the building, she had forgotten her awkwardness with Grady and relaxed. She didn't want to backslide into embarrassment. She'd had enough of that to last a lifetime.

"What will we look for inside?" she asked as she approached the door.

"We'll start in the cellar," he said as he unlocked the door and stood aside for her to enter.

She stepped inside and blinked against the sudden darkness. As her eyes adjusted to the dim light, she felt her heartbeat accelerate. Soon this would be her home. Right now it didn't look too impressive, but she had the ability to see past the graying plaster walls and cracked ceiling, past the ancient potbellied stove in the center of the dusty, cobwebbed room, past the grimy windows that kept the bright sun from lighting the dark interior.

There was promise here. The floorboards, though dirty and scuffed, were wide pine and she knew that if they were sanded and refinished they would glow with warmth. The ancient, cracking plaster walls and ceiling could be replaced, and the windows could be cleaned, allowing the bright sun to light the large central room.

Jennie walked forward slowly. At the back of the schoolroom there were two doors leading into two smaller rooms. She supposed they must have been cloakrooms or storage areas at one time. There was also an old staircase that led up to the attic. She wanted to investigate it right away, but then she remembered that Grady had said they would start downstairs.

When she turned to Grady, her eyes were glowing. "How do we get downstairs?" she asked.

"There's probably a staircase in one of these rooms." They entered the one on the right and discovered crude wooden steps descending into total darkness.

Jennie looked back at Grady doubtfully. "Um . . . after you, sir."

He grinned and drew a lighter from his pocket. "I should have brought a flashlight along. This will have to do, I guess." He held the small flame out over the first step. Jennie met his ironic gaze with a slightly squeamish look.

"Do I have to go down there too?"

"No," Grady said, laughing. "In fact, maybe you'd better stay up here in case the lighter runs out and I get lost down there. You'd have to go for help."

Jennie laughed, her eyes meeting Grady's in shared amusement. Then she was suddenly aware of just whom she was laughing with and the smile faltered on her face. This was the man she'd just made love with. How could she have forgotten?

"Look," she said, feeling suddenly awkward, "you go ahead. I'll just wander around up here." She gestured toward the schoolroom, but Grady made no move to go. She laughed in embarrassment. "Well? Aren't you going? Are you afraid of the dark?"

"No," he said softly, staring at her. "I'm just seeing the light."

She looked away quickly, at once embarrassed and pleased by his words. She hid her feelings behind flippancy. "Well, you can stand around if you want to, but *my* time is valuable!" With that, she whirled around and stalked out of the smaller room into the classroom. Behind her, Grady's low chuckle echoed in the dusty cloakroom. Then she heard his footsteps slowly descend the rickety steps.

As she wandered around the schoolroom, her thoughts were unfocused. She reached out to touch the potbellied stove and her hand came away grimy from years of dust and soot. Wiping her hand on her damp jeans, she smiled to herself. Perhaps that dunk in the pond had come in handy. At least she had a way of cleaning her hands after looking through all the cobwebs.

Sauntering toward a window, she rubbed a spot clean and stood peering out. From downstairs there came tuneless whistling and the dim echoes of thumpings, poundings, and taps. Jennie smiled to herself and wondered what Grady would do if she tapped back at him. She suspected that he'd laugh. There was nothing stuffy about Grady O'Hara. For all his virility—and there was plenty of that—there was a boyishness about him, a zest for living that was contagious. Jennie didn't know when she'd had such a good time as she was having this afternoon.

Then all that had happened by the pond came back to her and she felt embarrassment and humiliation again. How could she be standing here thinking what a good time she was having? Why did she keep forgetting her unforgivable behavior? She stood and looked out the peephole she had cleaned in the grimy window, brooding over those questions.

It was as if she were two different people. One was the usual Jennie Winters, the one who was comfortable with Dana Avery, the businesswoman with the sharp mind and cutting tongue. But now there was this other, newer Jennie. A Jennie who could be swept off her feet by a stranger and allow herself to be made love to within minutes of meeting him; a Jennie who found herself laughing into that same man's eyes and thrilling to his easily murmured words that he had "seen the light." This Jennie, the new one, felt as fresh as spring, and filled with laughter. Everything interested her—Grady O'Hara most of all. This Jennie found she liked hiking through the woods and examining foundations and roofs. This Jennie, in fact, seemed to like anything that involved being with Grady O'Hara.

But could this Jennie be trusted? Who was she really? Sighing, Jennie leaned her forehead against the cool surface of the glass and tried to block out her thoughts. It was too much to take in and assimilate at once. The entire afternoon was mind-boggling, and she would need time and distance to put it all into perspective. For now she would try to rein in her unruly behavior and keep anything else from happening between her and Grady.

The sound of Grady's footsteps trudging slowly up the steps brought Jennie out of her reverie. Straightening, she turned her head and saw his wide-shouldered frame fill the doorway.

Her heart seemed to stop for a fraction of a second; then it burst into a staccato beat. Seeing him was like seeing the sun after days of clouds. He filled her with light. She drank him in as if he were water and she had been out in the heat too long. The top four buttons of his denim shirt were unbuttoned, allowing the wiry dark hairs on his chest to spill out, and Jennie remembered with almost painful clarity how those hairs had pressed against her breasts, how her nipples had grazed there, hardening under the warm pressure of his skin.

Raising her eyes, Jennie saw that he was staring at her. Suddenly it was like it had been at the pond all over again. An electric current seemed to crackle in the air between them, drawing them irresistibly together. Without thinking, Jennie moved toward Grady, then stopped herself. Faltering, she stared at him as her pulse pounded erratically. She realized with dismay that her nipples were swelling, as if she were once again experiencing his touch.

But she mustn't. She must not let it happen again. Breaking eye contact, she sought sanity in light conversation.

"Is everything all right in the cellar? No rotting timbers or missing supports?"

At first she thought he wasn't going to reply; then he nodded, his eyes locking on hers. "Everything's fine," he said, his voice low and husky.

The quality in his voice sent shivers along her spine. It was the tone a lover used, low and urgent and filled with an underlying throbbing. It was the kind of tone that seduced a woman if she wasn't careful.

But Jennie was going to be careful. She had to be. There would be no more repetitions of this afternoon. Whirling around, she walked to the window and stared out, biting down hard on her lip to distract her from Grady's disturbing presence.

"Then the schoolhouse is structurally sound?" she asked, her voice unnaturally loud.

Grady didn't answer. Instead, he approached her slowly. She stood at the window and stared straight ahead, trying to pretend she was interested in the view, but every part of her was attuned to the man advancing on her. He came to a stop so close to her that she could almost feel his breath. The heat from his body seemed to envelop her, and she felt her senses wavering under the onslaught of his nearness. She swallowed hard and kept staring out the window, her body rigid from her effort to keep it in control.

"The schoolhouse is fine, Jennie," Grady said quietly. "If that's what's worrying you."

"No, I . . . I mean, *yes*. I mean . . ." She broke off, unable to find an explanation for her behavior. The silence stretched between them, filled by the sudden pounding of Jennie's heartbeat as it echoed in her ears like a pagan drum. She wondered wildly if Grady heard it too. She felt as if she were bound by silken cord, trapped by her awareness of the man who stood so close behind her.

"Well, if it's not the schoolhouse that's worrying you, what is it, Jennie?"

If he wanted an answer, she thought irritably, then he shouldn't ask questions in that sexy voice. It totally incapacitated her and she felt helpless to respond. If she spoke, she knew her voice would crack and betray her. All she could do was stare out the window and try to keep her legs from collapsing.

"Well?" Grady insisted softly.

She closed her eyes and leaned her forehead against the cool glass, praying that he would leave her alone. But he wouldn't. As if reading her mind, he reached out a hand and slid it up her arm, letting it rest at the crook of her elbow. When he rubbed his thumb over the soft skin, she almost moaned in ecstasy, but Jennie caught her bottom lip between her teeth and stopped herself in time.

"Jennie." His voice was hypnotic, low and soft and urgent all at once. "Jennie, turn around."

Frantic to break the tension, she whirled around and tried to brush past him, but he still held her arm. She reached out to ward him off, but instead her hands came up against the warm surface of his sun-bronzed chest.

"Ohhh," she murmured breathlessly, her eyes once again trapped by his. She stood there caught in the invisible web he wove. Staring up into those incredible blue eyes, Jennie thought she would drown in them, and she felt all her resolve drain away under the magic he worked.

They might have stood that way for minutes, oblivious of everything but each other, when Grady's hand tightened on her arm and she felt him drawing her inexorably toward him. It was like falling into space. All her moorings were gone and she floated free, watching his lips come down to meet hers as if in slow motion. If she didn't act soon, he would kiss her and then she would truly be lost.

She must act. His eyes were boring into hers, mesmerizing her like a frightened rabbit, and his lips were drawing ever closer. She must act. Shaking her head soundlessly, she tore her arm from his grip and pushed past him, running from the schoolroom out into the crystalline air.

Drawing a huge breath, she stood and lifted her eyes. The blue sky looked anemic next to Grady's eyes. Never, never again would she see blue and not think of Grady O'Hara. And from now on she would always pity the sky, so pale in comparison with his magnificent eyes.

# Chapter Five

❧

*Jennifer Elizabeth Winters.* Jennie signed her name on the mortgage agreement with swift, sure strokes, then looked up at the solemn faces around the impressive oak table. Her lawyer, Dana Avery's lawyer, and Dana Avery himself all sat watching her.

"Ah!" Dana Avery's lawyer broke the silence with a hearty laugh. "The deed is done, then!" His beefy face grew even more red. "No pun intended, of course!"

There were murmured chuckles from the men and then the sound of chairs scraping back on the parquet floor as everyone rose. Jennie stood and straightened her navy-and-white dress. She wore navy-blue slingback heels and carried a navy leather bag. Around her neck she wore a red-and-white silk scarf.

Her lawyer turned to her and held out his hand. "Ms. Winters, I wish you the best of luck."

"Mr. Davis. Thank you." She shook his hand, smiling as he murmured a conventional phrase, and then she was free. She turned and walked out of the office. The Connecticut air was humid, but Jennie looked and felt fresh and alive.

She had done it. She had bought the schoolhouse! Inside she was shaking, but she was proud that she was outwardly calm. Still, the hardest task awaited her. She was going to meet Grady O'Hara this afternoon at the schoolhouse, and he would give her his written agreement to do the constuction work. After consulting with three other contractors, she realized that Grady was the best man. He had given her a competitive bid and everyone she'd spoken to in the community had recommended him without hesitation.

But the thought of working with Grady still daunted her. She had seen him last weekend when they had met briefly so he could give her a detailed bid, and she still felt her stomach swirl at the thought of those clear blue eyes. He'd been all business, and had hardly looked at her, his mind clearly on his work.

But Jennie had certainly noticed *him*, and that was what bothered her. Since that first meeting three weeks ago, she hadn't been able to get him out of her mind. Even at work in her Hartford office she would find herself pausing over a memo, her thoughts flying back to that clear, sunny afternoon by the pond and the incredible moments they had spent there. Then her cheeks would grow heated and she would rip up the memo in anger and start over again, only to have the same thing happen the next day, and the next, and then the next.

No, it wasn't Grady she was worried about. It was her own powerful reaction to him that disturbed her. Never before had a man gotten under her skin this way, and she was determined to hold him at bay.

She was just fitting the key in her car door when she

heard Dana Avery call her name. She turned her head to see him hurrying toward her.

"Ms. Winters, I'm glad I caught up with you."

Jennie smiled at him. He returned the smile, revealing teeth any dentist would be proud to boast about. "Look, I was wondering if you'd like to have lunch with me in Sturbridge. We could go to the Publick House and celebrate your new home."

Jennie hesitated. It was Friday. She had taken a room in a Sturbridge motel for the weekend and planned to drive back there now and grab something for lunch before meeting Grady at the schoolhouse. The more she thought about it, the more it seemed a perfect idea. She could lunch with Dana and get to know him. Perhaps he would eclipse Grady. She had to work with Grady, after all, and so she wanted to keep things on a strictly business level between them. That edict didn't extend to Dana Avery.

Smiling, Jennie nodded. "That sounds fine. I was just on my way there anyway."

Dana's smile fell. "Oh. Then I can't convince you to ride with me?" He half-turned and indicated a Jaguar near her car.

She smiled but shook her head. "Sorry. I've got to change so I can head for the schoolhouse after lunch."

He shrugged and held her car door open for her, then slammed it shut when she had slid behind the wheel. "See you at the Publick House, then."


"To you and the schoolhouse." Dana Avery held up his martini glass in a toast. Jennie smiled and touched her wineglass to his. "To the schoolhouse," she murmured, and took a sip of her chablis.

Dana Avery watched her admiringly. "I think I'm going to like having you around Stockton. It's gotten a little boring in the last few years."

Jennie smiled into her glass. "You mean ever since your wife left?" she asked, her eyes dancing with mischief.

Dana's smile faltered. "Why . . . er . . . no. No, that's not what I meant at all." He was so confused that a faint blush crept up from beneath his collared neck and tinged his skin pink.

Jennie stared at him. Didn't he have a sense of humor at all? She decided to give him the benefit of the doubt. The wine and the antique decor of the restaurant were relaxing her. It was pleasant here and the company was no worse than most of the men she had dated. She leaned on her hand and smiled into his eyes.

"So what's so boring about Stockton?" she asked softly. "And why didn't you warn me before I bought the schoolhouse?"

He seemed to be able to cope with this kind of banter. Relaxing, he smiled at her. "Oh, you know—same old faces. It's just that yours is refreshingly new and pretty."

Jennie smiled at the compliment, running her finger around the rim of her wineglass. She sat and wondered briefly why it didn't bother her to flirt with Dana Avery, yet the thought of seeing Grady sent her stomach into somersaults. She supposed it was because she was so used to men like Dana, so used to automatically falling into a light, flirtatious banter that she did it without thinking. Grady was another matter. She had never met anyone like him before and didn't know how to respond.

But enough of thinking of Grady, she reminded herself. She forced herself to talk to Dana. "What do you do, Mr. Avery?"

"Please. Call me Dana."

She smiled in assent. "Dana, then."

"I own an insurance agency."

"I see. Mrs. Peevy mentioned that your family's been in this area for quite some time."

"Yes, we go back a couple hundred years. Avery Corners in Pomfret is named after my great-grandfather. Avery Junction just outside Putnam is my grandfather's doing." He smiled at her. "We're an old and respected family in eastern Connecticut." He shifted his chair closer to Jennie's. "But let's not talk about my family. Let's talk about you."

Jennie focused on her wineglass. "What do you want to know, Dana?" She felt her pleasure in the luncheon draining away rapidly. She didn't know what it was about Dana Avery, but she felt she could anticipate almost everything he did and said. Jennie wondered if he had ever done anything just for sheer pleasure. He seemed to be the kind of man who went through life doing exactly what was expected of him. Why did that bother Jennie? Hadn't she always been conventional and proper, worrying about what others would think? Yes—until she had seen the schoolhouse. Then something had happened to her. She smiled to herself. Her friends and family had said she'd gone mad. Only Grady had encouraged her.

At the thought of Grady, Jennie felt a shiver glide over her skin. She took a quick sip of wine and tried to concentrate on what Dana was saying.

". . . and what intrigues me is that we probably have an awful lot in common."

Jennie heard those last words and realized that he couldn't have chosen anything more calculated to turn her off.

"Do you think so?" she asked, cocking her head sideways as she considered him. He was extremely handsome, very polished, and obviously well-to-do. Why did she dislike having things in common with Dana Avery? Could it be because he was safe and unthreatening? It felt strange to realize that he was everything she had once thought she wanted in a man. Now she was beginning to wonder if she knew exactly what she did want.

Dana smiled his perfect smile. "I'll bet if we do some investigating, we'll find we have a lot in common."

Jennie sipped her wine, then murmured something innocuous.

"In fact," he said, "while I was watching you sign those mortgage papers, I was thinking of something else entirely."

"Were you?" Jennie glanced at him inquiringly.

"Yes, I was thinking that I'd like to get to know you better, Jennie. I'd like to take you out."

Jennie leaned on her hand and smiled. "Well, we have insurance in common. We could sit around all night and discuss actuarial statistics. Or underwriting. Now, *that's* interesting stuff."

"I wasn't thinking of insurance, Jennie."

"No?" she asked, cocking an ironic eyebrow.

He pulled his chair closer and reached for her hand. "How about going to dinner with me tonight? If you think lunch is good here, you should see dinner."

Jennie slid her hand from his grasp. His palm wasn't sweaty, he had a good, firm, masculine hand, but she could find nothing about Dana Avery that was exciting. He left her cold, and after being with Grady O'Hara, she realized that she never wanted to be left cold by a man again.

"I'm really sorry, Dana, but I've already made plans for tonight."

"Tomorrow night, then."

She smiled to soften her words. "Tomorrow night's busy also."

"Sunday?"

She laughed softly. "Sunday I'm working at the schoolhouse and then driving home."

"I'll follow you home. We can go to dinner in Hartford."

One thing could be said for Dana Avery—he was persistent. She hadn't been pursued like this since college. "No, Dana," she said firmly. "I'll have to get ready for work."

He sat back, and she noticed that he pushed his chair away just a fraction. She smiled to herself. Perhaps that meant that he was going to stop asking her out.

The rest of the lunch was predictable. They talked about work, politics, and their families. The only time Jennie found her interest warming was when he mentioned his children. That seemed to encourage him, so he spent the rest of the meal talking about them and ended it by asking her to come over and meet them sometime.

She nodded and smiled. "I will, Dana, as soon as things settle down a bit. Grady tells me it's going to be hectic for a while."

Dana shrugged. "But that's what you hired *him* for,"

he protested. "Let him do the worrying. You can come out on weekends and see how things are progressing, then drive over to my place and we can have a game of tennis." He eyed her speculatively. "I'll bet you play well."

As a matter of fact, she did, and she smiled at the thought. "Afraid tennis is out this summer—I'm going to be working right alongside Grady."

"*What?*" Dana laughed incredulously. "Why in God's name do you want to do that? Let him do the grunt work, that's what you're paying him for."

Jennie found her temper rising, but she controlled it admirably. Dabbing the napkin at her lips, she placed it on the table and slid back her chair to stand up. "It just so happens that I want to help out, Dana. It's my new home and I'm rather excited about fixing it up." She smiled, but it was no longer warm. "Thank you for lunch. It was delightful."

They walked to her car together and said good-bye; then Jennie heaved a sigh of relief as she slid behind the wheel and headed for her motel room. Once in the cool air-conditioned room, she let her temper flare. Unzipping her dress, she stepped out of it and flung it across the bed.

"Grunt work! That's what you're paying him for!" Jennie flung off her shoes and kicked them toward the closet. "How dare he talk like that!"

She tried to pretend that Dana's attitude angered her because he made light of her working along with Grady, but deep inside she knew it was something else that was bothering her. Something that had been lying just under the surface ever since she met Grady: he was a carpenter.

Jennie stood and stared at her image in the mirror, realizing that she was more like Dana Avery than she cared to admit: conventional, doing what was expected of her, always dating the "right" men, going to the "right" places, the "in" spots. Looking at herself with critical eyes, she wondered what Grady O'Hara had ever seen to make him want to make love to her. Then she snorted in self-contempt. Wasn't it obvious? He was a man and he'd found himself in the fortunate position of being alone with a willing woman. Any man would have taken advantage and gone as far as he could. But if she were honest with herself, Jennie had to admit that that wasn't what was bothering her.

No, Grady was an attractive man and she was an attractive woman and they had come together spontaneously in a way that had brought Jennie more joy than she had ever experienced with a man. Then why couldn't she just accept it and let it go at that? Why did she feel so embarrassed by it all?

She realized now that it had something to do with him, yes, but it mostly had to do with his work. He wasn't "right" for her. He was a *carpenter*, for heaven's sake! And she was a professional woman, an executive in an insurance company—that most conservative bastion of the financial community.

She smiled bitterly at the thought of how her colleagues would react if she showed up at a cocktail party with Grady in tow. His muscled torso would catch every woman's eye, and there would be refined welcomes and well-mannered chitchat about building homes and questions about how he *ever* got started in such an exciting career. Jennie winced at the thought, knowing that after they left, the tongues would start to wag, and the consensus would be that Jennie was getting to "that age" when a woman badly needed a man. *Obviously* Grady O'Hara was spectacular in bed and of *course* that explained it. . . .

Jennie flopped down on the bed and lay staring disconsolately at the ceiling. Wasn't that precisely what she feared about her and Grady—that their relationship was based purely on physical attraction.

She lay there a few minutes, then dragged herself to the closet and eyed her clothes sourly. Designer jeans. Designer T-shirts. Designer sandals. Everything calculated to tell the world that Jennie Winters knew what to buy, Jennie had the money to buy it, and Jennie had style.

"Ugh!" She wished she could throw everything out and pull on a frumpy pair of overalls and an old plaid shirt and tell the world to go to hell. Sighing, she wiggled out of her panty hose and pulled on a pair of the designer jeans. These at least made her smile. While they weren't the same pair she had worn three weeks ago when she had fallen into the pond, they were similar. She wondered if Grady would notice.

She shrugged into a T-shirt and combed her hair, then tied it back with a blue ribbon. Slipping into high-heeled sandals, she set off for Stockton and the schoolhouse.

Thirty minutes later, Jennie stood in front of her new home, knee-deep in a tangle of weeks and grass. The sky was pale blue and cloudless, the maples and oaks were in full leaf, and robins called raucously from the branches. Day lilies grew in great clumps along the stone wall that fronted the road, and farther down the road an old tractor grunted along as it plowed a field.

Jennie sighed contentedly as she gazed at the school-house with glowing eyes. The front door was tilted at an odd angle in its frame. The red paint was chipping and faded, flaking off in places to expose the bare wood beneath. The windows were grimy and one pane in a front window had been broken at some time and then patched with cardboard that had grown soft and moldly from repeated drenchings in the rain. The wooden stoop under the front door sagged precariously. It was, she decided, a mess, but it was the most beautiful mess she had ever seen.

Looking up through the maple branches, Jennie hugged herself with excitement, then turned at the sound of a grumbling motor. From around the bend, Grady O'Hara's four-wheel-drive pickup appeared. It was old. No, Jennie amended, it was ancient. She had seen it for the first time last weekend and it had quite literally taken her breath away when she rode in it from Grady's place to the schoolhouse. It rattled. It shook. It bounced. The passenger door was tied closed with wire and she had had to get in on Grady's side and slide across a torn and patched seat, only to find that she couldn't put her feet on the floor because there was a hole in the floorboards. Grady had taken care of that by putting a battered red cooler on the floor over the hole, and so she had sat with her feet propped on top of the cooler filled with Canadian ale, her hands folded in her lap as she bounced in the seat. There were tools scattered in the back of the pickup, and every time the truck bounced over a rut, they rattled and shifted and banged around like teeth in an old man's mouth. The muffler, or what was left of it, no longer muffled, and the paint had darkened to a grimy navy blue.

The truck rattled to a stop and Jennie saw that Kaiser's head was sticking out of the passenger window, his great tongue lolling out contentedly. He barked when he saw her, then decided to jump out the window and come bounding across the yard as Grady got out of the truck.

"Down, Kaiser," Jennie said, grabbing the dog's paws as he stood up and tried to lick her face. She grimaced and pushed him down and wished he hadn't taken such a great liking to her. Since that afternoon by the pond, when she had fallen in and then pushed Grady in, Kaiser seemed to think that Jennie wanted to do nothing but play. Jennie patted Kaiser on the head, then looked up as Grady approached. At the sight of him, her heart lurched and she felt her face brighten with a smile. It was preposterous, but she felt as excited as a first-grader at recess.

Grady's eyes met hers in an answering smile that almost took her breath away; then he stood and looked her up and down, shaking his head back and forth in exaggerated resignation.

"When are you city-slicker girls every going to learn?" he asked. He was grinning at her, and she couldn't help responding to him. She lifted her chin obstinately and glared at him.

"What's *that* supposed to mean, *farmboy*?"

His grin widened as he tilted his head to the side and ran his eyes up and down her figure. "You think those are *working* clothes, dude?"

She looked down at herself. "Sure. They're *jeans*, aren't they?"

"*Jeans?* You call those things *jeans*?" Grady's rich laughter filled the air. "My God, Jennie Winters, have I got a lot to teach you."

Jennie looked at Kaiser and folded her arms, directing her words to the dog. "I see your master's a *couturier* now, Kaiser. Not only does he hammer and saw, he plans milady's wardrobe."

Grady's shoulders shook with silent laughter as he produced a bottle of champagne from behind his back. "*And* milady's menu."

Jennie stared at the bottle, an expensive French import; then she raised her eyes to Grady. "What's this?"

"There—you see? I *told* you I had a lot to teach you. It's champagne, mademoiselle. To celebrate the recent purchase of this sorry property."

"*Sorry?*" Jennie's temper went off like a rocket. "You're the one who told me it was damned solid and a good piece of property to buy. You went around with that awl of yours and tested every damn post and beam for dry rot, then stomped all over that confounded roof, not to mention hunkering all over the place on the ground to get a look at the foundation, and *you* have the gall to call my new home sorry?"

Grady held up a conciliatory hand. "Okay, okay. *I'm* sorry. How's that?"

Jennie felt her hackles slip back into place. "That's better." She looked at him and felt a grin begin to tremble at her lips. She fought it valiantly, but then had to give in. She reached for the champagne and examined the label, then raised an eyebrow.

"I'm impressed."

"How impressed?"

She made a back-and-forth motion with her hand. "So-so."

Grady took the bottle from her. "Then the first lesson starts right now: You should be *very* impressed. This is

Dom Perignon. It's an outstanding vintage and it's pretty rare. Here." He handed her the bottle and started off toward the truck. "I'll get the glasses."

Jennie stared after him. Glasses? Astounding, she thought as she watched him lean into the truck and pull out a wicker basket. When he walked back toward her, she could hear the sound of glass tinkling beneath the wicker lid. It was so incongruous to see him carrying a wicker picnic basket that she couldn't think of anything to say. She watched mutely as he knelt in the grass, which by now was thoroughly trampled down, and removed the lid. He took out two fluted champagne glasses and set them on the ground, then whipped out a checkered cotton tablecoth and shook it out on the grass. He looked up at Jennie and grinned.

"Close your mouth, Jennie Winters, you'll let in flies."

She knelt down beside him and peered into the basket. Inside were a wedge of cheese, some imported crackers, two highly polished apples, two pears, a bunch of grapes, a tiny loaf of freshly baked bread, a small crock of butter, a Delftware-handled knife, and, finally, two checked napkins to match the tablecloth.

"Inspection finished?" Grady asked, sounding amused.

Jennie sat back on her heels and stared at him with unbelieving eyes. "What *is* this?" she asked. "S. S. Pierce?"

He shook his head. "No. Fortnum and Mason." He gently took the bottle from her hands and wrapped one of the napkins around the neck; then he tore off the foil and began to work the cork away from the bottle. There was a delicate pop as the cork came out and a thin wisp of vapor escaped. He filled one of the glasses halfway and handed it to her, then filled the other glass, set the bottle down, and held up his glass in a toast.

"To your new home, Jennie. May it bring you great happiness."

Jennie was deeply moved. She couldn't help remembering Dana's toast at lunch. The contrast between their words was as great as the difference between the two men. How odd that it was Grady, a carpenter, who had chosen the most wonderful way to welcome her to her new home.

She held up her glass and clinked it against Grady's, then sipped the champagne. The bubbles tickled her nose and she grinned in delight. "Mmm, this is *good!*"

"Try some cheese and bread, milady." Grady broke off a piece of bread, cut a slab of cheese to go with it, and handed it to her. She bit into it and chewed happily, then washed it down with more champagne and grinned at him.

"Well?" he said. "Don't I get any thanks?"

"Oh!" She put her hand to her mouth in embarrassment. "Thank you, Grady, it's wonderful. Everything. I . . . I—" She broke off when she saw that he was shaking his head back and forth. She tilted her head inquiringly. "What?"

"Jennie, Jennie, Jennie," he said softly, still shaking his head at her. "When a man brings you champagne, you don't thank him with words."

Jennie stared speechlessly at him, afraid to ask what he meant. But then he was taking her glass from her nerveless fingers and setting it down beside his own. He moved toward her and took her chin gently in his hand as his indigo eyes caught and held hers.

"When a man brings you champagne, Jennie Winters," he said softly, "you give him a kiss in return."

Mesmerized, she watched as his lips descended; then her eyelids fluttered down and she felt his arms go around her, pulling her up against his brawny chest. Jennie melted against him, aware of a floodtide of warmth filling her. His lips gently took hers, and she was aware of the taste of champagne before she was caught up in a whirlwind, lost in his embrace.

# Chapter Six

❧

The whirlwind let her down too quickly. Grady drew away and Jennie's eyes flew open in protest. He was watching her with amused eyes.

"That was your second lesson, Ms. Winters," he said softly.

"What's the third?" she whispered, feeling drugged by his incredible blue eyes.

He broke into a grin, but didn't answer. Standing up unexpectedly, Grady leaned down to take her hand and pull her up. Suddenly he was all business.

"The third lesson," he said briskly, "is your clothes."

"My clothes?" Jennie felt betrayed. She had wanted the kiss to go on and on, but here she was getting a lecture on how to dress instead. She whipped her hand out of his, feeling suddenly angry. "What's wrong with my clothes?" she demanded heatedly.

He looked her up and down and seemed about to answer, when he paused and took a closer look at her jeans. "Those jeans look familiar. Are they the ones that ended up in my pond?"

So he *had* remembered! Jennie tossed her head haughtily. "No, they just look like them."

"What happened to the others?"

"They shrank," she said testily, folding her arms and fixing him with crackling, amber-flecked eyes.

A grin hovered at one corner of his mouth. "Not while you were still in them, I hope."

"No, luckily I got them off in time," she said airily. "Then I sat around all night watching them get smaller and smaller. They ended up a girl's size six-X and I gave them to my niece."

He gave a hoot of laughter that almost made her laugh too, but she resisted the impulse.

"And is your niece wearing them now?" he asked when his laughter had died away.

"No. Actually, they're still shrinking." If she was going to tell a tall tale, she reasoned, then it may as well be *really* tall. "The last I heard, she put them on a Barbie doll and poor Barbie cracked when they continued to shrink. Word has it that my niece is aiming for an entry in *The Guinness Book of World Records*—world's smallest designer jeans. She's hoping they'll end up small enough to fit into a thimble."

While she spoke, Grady put his head back and roared with laughter. Jennie could resist no longer; her own laughter bubbled up, escalating from helpless giggles to rib-holding guffaws. She had to hold her sides in pain as she lost control, and it didn't help that Grady was still laughing. At the same time, Kaiser started running around the schoolhouse, barking frantically. It was a small zone of pandemonium that ended only when Kaiser spied a rabbit and took off pell-mell after it, his barks dying out as he sped across the countryside in pursuit.

The sudden quiet in the schoolyard was broken only by gasps and sighs from both Grady and Jennie. They settled down on the ground and Grady grinned at her.

"What really happened?"

"They shrank," she said with an answering smile. "I had to throw them out."

Grady's easy laughter held a companionable quality that warmed Jennie completely. She lay back on the ground and looked up at the sky feeling as if she could stay here forever. It would be wonderful to loll in the shade of the towering maple, her head pillowed on the fresh-scented grass, and while away her days like this. It was a new experience for her. Being city-bred, she was used to sidewalks and tiny patches of manicured lawns. The country and all its delights was proving to be good medicine. The peace alone was worth the price of the schoolhouse. Only Kaiser's distant barking and the birds in the trees broke the silence, and the wildflowers and grass combined in a heavenly scent that was like sweet perfume after the diesel bus fumes and industrial pollution of the city.

And then there was Grady. Jennie had never shared such companionable silence with a man. She had always felt compelled to make a witty comment when she was with a man, and silence had seemed a sign of failure, that things weren't going well. Now she was so relaxed she felt no compelling need to speak.

This too was a revelation. If she didn't find him so overpoweringly attractive, she would think of him as a friend. There was that quality already between them— the ability to talk, to share laughter and be silent together.

But Grady broke the spell by standing up and tower-

ing over her. "Come on, lazybones," he said, reaching
down to take her hand and pull her up. "We've got
Lesson Three to go over."

Jennie gave him a provocative smile. "Oh, heck! I
was kinda hoping it's be taught horizontally."

Grady's eyes flared for a moment; then he dropped
her hand and stood back. "No way, Jennie Winters. If I
get horizontal with you, it won't be Lesson Three I give
you."

She looked away quickly, acutely conscious of him as
a man. She wondered what devil had possessed her to
tease him, even for a moment. Hadn't she just found
out that when he kissed her she was helpless to fight
him? If she wanted things to remain on a business
footing, she'd best follow his lead. She looked back at
him and had the uncomfortable feeling that he was
reading her mind. But if he was, he didn't needle her.
Though his eyes were lit with laughter, he launched into
a discussion of what they would do in the next few
weeks.

"First of all," he was saying, "we'll tear out the plaster
ceilings and walls, then we'll clean the place out. That
calls for comfortable clothes—"

"Oh-oh," Jennie interrupted. "Sounds like Lesson
Three coming up."

"Precisely. When you work on a construction site,
Jennie, you need clothes that are easy to move around
in and that give you some protection."

"Protection?"

"Definitely. If you dropped a hunk of plaster on your
foot right now," he said, pointing to her high-heeled,
open-toed sandals, "you'd break a toe. And you could
stumble off those stilts of yours."

"Stilts!" She bristled angrily, but he ignored her and went on.

"You could turn your ankle or, even worse, break it. You're going to be doing a lot of bending, stooping, and lifting. That means loose-fitting jeans and shirts. The best clothes are workman's clothes, carpenter's jeans or overalls, and a long-sleeved cotton shirt. And get a pair of gloves. You don't want any splinters or nails going through that soft skin of yours."

Mollified, Jennie nodded. "I guess you're right. Anything else?"

He softened his lecture with a smile. "Yeah," he said softly, reaching out to touch the brown hair that cascaded down her back. "Tie this pretty stuff up on your head or I'll be hitting my thumb with the hammer every five seconds."

Her eyes warmed to his, as she found herself smiling. "And why would you do that, Mr. O'Hara?" she asked softly.

"Because I'd be looking at you and not at the nail, Ms. Winters."

They stood and looked into each other's eyes for a moment longer; then Jennie turned away. Her skin was tingling from the look they had exchanged and she knew her eyes were glowing. She realized she'd have to find something to say soon or she'd be in danger of breaking into song and executing an elated two-step. She was saved when her eyes fell on the forgotten picnic basket.

"Hey!" she exclaimed. "We forgot the food!"

Grady sat down on the tablecloth. "Not to mention the drink." He poured more champagne into her glass, then filled his own and set the bottle down. He took papers out of his pocket and handed them to her. "This is the written agreement, Jennie. Why don't you look it over and see if everything's all right with you."

In the space of a second they had gone from pleasure to business. Jennie took the papers and began reading. She knew the agreement was important. If something were to happen between her and Grady and he didn't fulfill his obligations, this agreement was all she'd have to fall back on. The potential difficulties of being personally involved with a man who worked for her was borne in on her again, and she immediately sobered. She concentrated on the words of the agreement, and when she had finished reading, she was satisfied that it was a sound contract.

"This looks fine," she said. "But do you really think it will all be done by Labor Day? That's only a couple months away."

"If everything runs as scheduled, it will be," Grady assured her. "Of course, there are always setbacks on construction projects, but for the most part I think it will run smoothly. The electrician is set to come out on Monday to install the service entrance. If he shows up, we'll be in business."

"*If* he shows up?"

Grady grinned. "That's the hardest part to plan on. Subcontractors are notoriously independent. If something else comes along, he may decide not to come on Monday. But I've selected a good man who's pretty reliable, so I'm not too worried."

"And what's a service entrance?"

"That's what's called a construction service entrance. It means that the electrician will put in the meter and a fuse box and some outlets for my power tools. Then by

Tuesday or Wednesday, if we get the plaster down and if the utility company gets the poles up and the lines strung in to the property, we'll be in business. The plumber can install a water pump and a line from the well. He'll put in an outside faucet so we'll have water. When you decide where you want the bathroom and kitchen fixtures, then he'll be able to run the water lines into the house." He shifted closer, producing the pad he'd been sketching on. "Here are the preliminary sketches. I recommend tearing out the cloakroom walls completely and redoing it like this."

Jennie studied the sketches as excitement bubbled up inside her. Grady seemed to have caught exactly what she wanted.

"Oh, Grady," she said fervently. "These are *good*." She held the sketches out at arm's length, then looked at him. "Why, you're really talented!"

"That's why you hired me, isn't it?" he asked, his eyes gleaming.

"I hired you, Mr. O'Hara," she said with mock sternness, "because I heard from everyone in Stockton that you're a good carpenter and that you work well with old buildings. I had no idea you were an artist and an architect as well."

"It seems to me, Ms. Winters," he answered softly, "that there's an awful lot you don't know about me."

Jennie's eyes fell from his as her face flamed with color. Grady ignored her chagrin and pointed to the floor plan. "Here's how I see the first floor. It's all essentially one big room, with the living area separated from the kitchen by the hearth for a wood stove. The kitchen will open out onto the sunroom, which can serve as a dining area or a garden room, whatever you prefer. The bathroom will be over here to the right, on the other side of the staircase that leads up to the sleeping loft."

"It's beautiful," she breathed. "Oh, I'm so excited!"

Grady put the plan to one side and produced a drawing of the living room that showed his plan to remove part of the existing ceiling to make a cathedral ceiling, leaving the back part of the attic over the kitchen and the bathroom as a sleeping loft.

"This makes it real," Jennie said after she had looked over the sketch. "Before, it was all in my head. I've been lying in bed at night trying to picture it all, but sometimes when I get here and see how ramshackle it looks, I get afraid that I've bitten off more than I can chew."

Grady shook his head. "No way, Jennie. The structure of the schoolhouse is solid. Because of the post-and-beam construction, there aren't any load-bearing partitions, so we can just gut the interior and start from there. We'll insulate the outside walls, then put up the rough framing. Then the electrician can finish the wiring and we can install either wallboard or a good wood paneling. These are the things you're going to have to think about—where you want the electrical outlets in each room, whether you want wood paneling or painted walls, that sort of thing."

"There's just so much!"

"It's a big job redoing a house, but you're luckier than most. This place is small, and essentially it's only one big room. Most people who buy Victorians or Colonials end up having to redo one room at a time. That can drag on for years."

"Well, at least I've already decided a few things. I

want painted white walls with stripped woodwork and floors. I love the look of natural pine with white walls. With a few quilts hung on the walls and some pieces of folk art, the schoolhouse is going to be the most charming house in Stockton."

Grady grinned as he stretched out on the grass. "Just like a woman. Decorating already."

Jennie laughed. When Grady said it, it was a joke. If another man said it, it might sound like a slight against women. She glanced at him and saw that he had closed his eyes. Grinning to herself, she sat back against the maple tree and looked around, taking in the pure beauty of her surroundings.

Jennie knew this place would never lose its charm. As far as the eye could see, there was nothing but nature. Trees arched over the meandering country road that was bordered by stone walls overgrown by ferns and day lilies. The birds were plentiful, filling the air with song. In the tall grass and clover, there was a constant hum of bees and insects busy at work. The air was sweet with the mixed scents of flowers and wild herbs. Overhead the maple branches formed a green canopy that cast dappled sunlight on the ground.

It was, Jennie decided, a little bit of heaven. But her thoughts were interrupted by Grady's drowsy voice.

"Kaiser must have found the rabbit," he said. "I don't hear him barking anymore."

Jennie looked over at him. His eyes were still closed and she thought he was ready to drift off to sleep. "Does that mean he's gone for the rest of the afternoon?"

Grady smiled sleepily. "Mmm hmmm."

Jennie pulled her legs up and rested her chin on her knees to study Grady. She drank in the soft fall of his hair across his forehead, the sensual curve of his lips, the gentle rise and fall of his muscular chest. The dark hair that she remembered so well curled softly in the V opening of his chambray workshirt, bringing back memories of that other afternoon, just three weeks earlier.

It was incredible that she had made love with this man. They had laughed uproariously earlier, then pored over Grady's plans for the schoolhouse, and here they were resting in companionable silence. At no time had there been any of the embarrassment she'd felt after they had made love. It said a lot for Grady that he'd been able to help her relax with him. Three weeks ago she had thought that she'd never be able to work with him. Now she felt completely at ease.

She remembered the kiss he had given her earlier and amended her last thought. Well, not completely at ease—all she had to do was look at him to feel the pleasant ripples of arousal. Jennie knew she would have to fight that, for she was determined that there would be no repeat of the scene by the pond. She had spent years at TransContinental Insurance with the unwritten edict of not becoming involved with her co-workers. If it was important in business, it was even more important here. Grady worked for her, and she wanted nothing to jeopardize the renovation of her new home.

But as she looked at Grady again, Jennie couldn't help but think how full of surprises he was. The picnic basket and bottle of champagne were the kind of romantic gesture she never would have expected from a carpenter and general contractor, but he had taken the time to buy an expensive bottle of champagne and gather the ingredients for a perfect picnic. Either her stereotyped version of what a carpenter might do was wrong, or Grady wasn't a typical carpenter. Either way, she doubted she would ever come to a firm conclusion about him. He seemed a will-o'-the-wisp, incapable of being pinned down and analyzed. Just as Mrs. Peevy had once said, he was his own man. . . .

Just then Jennie heard the smooth purr of an engine and looked up to see Dana Avery's Jaguar approaching. She glanced over at Grady, who seemed to be asleep. She hissed at him in a low stage whisper. "Grady."

There was no response from him. "*Grady*," she said, louder this time. When he still didn't answer, she scrambled up from the ground and quickly dusted off her bottom. Dana's car had just coasted to a stop in front of the rock wall. What would he think when he saw all this? The picnic basket was spilling forth its lavish provisions onto the checked cloth, while bees hummed happily among the fruit and cheese, and Grady snored softly.

At that, Jennie did a double take. *Snoring?* Grady hadn't been snoring before! She reached over and shook his arm. "Grady!"

Did he stir? She bit her lip and cast a frenzied look back over her shoulder, then caught one corner of Grady's mouth tipping up into a grin.

"Grady O'Hara," she said, her voice clipped and efficient-sounding. "Dana Avery's here and I don't want him to see you sleeping like this. Now, get up!"

With his eyes still closed, Grady spoke out of one side of his mouth. "Why not? Have you got eyes for him? Do you think this might queer your pitch?"

"No, I do not have eyes for Dana Avery," she hissed. "Just get up and stop being such a hindrance."

"A hindrance to what?"

Jennie stuffed the crock of butter and the Delft-handled knife into the basket and crammed the lid on top. "To my getting this damned place straightened up. Now, come on, get *up*."

She tugged on the checked cloth, but it was firmly anchored beneath Grady's body. She gave a final beleaguered pull, then saw that Dana was climbing over the rock wall, and she let it go. Standing up, she hurriedly patted her hair. She was tempted to give Grady a swift kick, but resisted when she saw Dana bearing down on them. Grady had started snoring again. Livid with rage, she tried to plaster a pleasant look on her face when Dana approached.

"Why, Dana," she trilled. "How nice to see you!"

Grady's snoring momentarily sounded like a snort; then it smoothed out again into stentorian tones. Dana looked down at him; then his eyes swept the ground, taking in the checked cloth and the picnic basket and, finally, the fluted champagne glass still clutched in Grady's strong brown hand. When Dana looked up at Jennie, there was a mixture of dawning comprehension and censure in his eyes. It was exactly the look she had dreaded.

"I've come at a bad time, perhaps?" Dana asked delicately.

Jennie shook her head back and forth. "Why, no! Not at all!" She glanced at the picnic basket and smiled inanely. "In fact, you can help us finish the champagne." She stooped and threw back the lid on the basket and took out the bottle of champagne. "See? There's still a little left."

Dana smiled coolly. "Now I see why you couldn't stay long at lunch. You had bigger fish to fry."

Jennie thought she heard a satisfied purr somewhere within Grady's snore, but she put that out of her mind for the moment.

"Why, no! This was a surprise. Grady . . . I mean, Mr. O'Hara thought it all up by himself." Her smile suddenly faltered, and she followed Dana's eyes to look at Grady's sleeping form.

"Too much of the dog that bit him, I'd say," Dana remarked dryly, and Jennie smiled quickly in response.

She thought she heard a definite "harrumph" mingle with Grady's snoring, so she hurriedly poured some champagne and held her glass out to Dana.

"We were celebrating," she said lamely. 'Here, have some."

But Dana shook his head. "Actually, I just dropped by to see if I could persuade you to go out to dinner with me tomorrow evening." He looked from her to Grady and cocked an eyebrow. "But perhaps you're already occupied?"

"No." She gave a forced laugh, silently wishing she could kick Grady into Massachusetts. "But I'm afraid I can't, Dana. I start helping out here tomorrow morning. I'm going out this afternoon to buy some workclothes . . ." Did she hear a satisfied sound coming from Grady at that? "Then I'm going back to my motel room. It will be an early evening for me. Six A.M. comes awfully early, and I'm sure tomorrow evening I'll be dead tired."

"Six A.M.?" Dana laughed as if the time were preposterous. "Is that when you get up or start work?"

"That's when I plan on getting up. Grady wants me here by seven."

Grady's snoring was suddenly tapering off. Dana flicked

a glance toward him. "He's quite the taskmaster, isn't he?" he asked dryly.

She felt a sudden desire to defend Grady. Holding up the champagne bottle, she said, "Well, if he is, he sure knows what carrot to hold out."

From the ground came the sounds of Grady awakening. He yawned sleepily, then sat up and ran a hand through his hair. "Hello, Dana. Been here long?"

"A few moments," Dana said stiffly.

Grady looked at Jennie and smiled conspiratorially. "Still have some of that liquid sunshine?" he asked, indicating the bottle she still held.

She glared at him angrily. "Does the original Sunshine Boy need any?" she asked sarcastically.

His grin only infuriated her more. "No, but I was thinking Dana could use some." He looked at him with narrowed, critical eyes. "He looks awfully stiff in that navy-blue blazer and those freshly ironed pants. Maybe some champagne would help him unbend a little."

Dana stared at Grady coldly. "You always did think I was stiff, Grady, even when you worked for me that summer."

Jennie's eyes went quickly from Dana to Grady. There was something in the air that didn't feel right. When had Grady worked for Dana? And why was there so much tension between them?

"Yeah," Grady said easily. "And I believe I told you then that if you had unbent a little, your wife would have stayed with you."

Dana's jaw tightened. "I didn't think it was your place to comment on my marriage then, and I don't think it's your place now."

"But that's your problem, Dana—you're so stiff-necked you can't hear a man when he's got something important to say.''

"I hear you, Grady, but I don't like what I hear." Dana held himself ramrod straight, as if the tension that was suddenly in the air might harm him if he let down his guard. "Anyway," he added, "I'm sure Ms. Winters isn't interested in old business."

"Oh, you never know, Dana," Grady said easily. "You know women. If she's interested in you, you can bet she's all ears right about now."

When the conversation suddenly turned on her, Jennie cast a baleful eye on Grady. "Sometimes, Mr. O'Hara," she said tightly, "I think this champagne cork rightfully belongs in your big mouth."

He just grinned at her roguishly. "Anytime you want to stop me from speaking, Jennie Winters, you know exactly how to do it."

She felt embarrassed color creep up her neck and into her cheeks at the implication. Flicking a quick look at Dana, she saw that he was looking at her speculatively. Coupled with this picnic scene, Grady's words had planted a suspicion in his mind about her and Grady's relationship. While she wasn't interested in Dana, she didn't want Grady to know that, and his attitude only fueled her anger.

Raising her chin contentiously, she shot Grady an icy look, then smiled warmly at Dana. "I can't make it for dinner tomorrow evening, Dana, but perhaps we could make it in a few weeks."

Dana's face cleared. "Great! I'll stop by in a week or two and we can work it out then."

Jennie watched him walk back to his car, then turned

to find Grady's eyes on her. Her anger immediately bubbled up once again.

"I hope you're satisfied," she said icily. "That act you put on was first-class. The snoring alone would earn you an Academy Award."

He smiled and lay back on one elbow, his eyes lazily drifting over her figure. "Just giving Dana a run for his money, Jennie. We can't have him thinking you're all his just for the asking, can we? I thought you'd appreciate my helping out—making him jealous."

"The only help I need from you, Grady O'Hara, is written up in that agreement I just read. From now on, kindly limit yourself to carpentry work and general contracting."

Grady's eyes drifted downward over her figure once more, sending a tingling shiver over her skin; then he stood up and nodded. "Okay, Jennie. If that's the way you want it, from now on it will be strictly business between us."

She faltered for a moment. Was that the way she really wanted it? Staring at him, she raised her chin again and nodded curtly, then turned to gather up the remains of the picnic. It would be easier this way, she told herself; she'd worried enough about becoming further involved with a man who worked for her, and now she needn't worry any longer. And the way was cleared for Dana Avery to ask her out.

But as she covered the picnic basket, Jennie wondered if this was going the way she wanted it to. Wasn't it Grady she wanted, not Dana? And though she said she wanted to keep things strictly business between herself and Grady, her body was saying something else. Even now she was vividly aware of Grady's presence.

She remembered the way he had looked at her, the way he had kissed her just an hour ago, and wondered with a pang if she really knew what she was doing.

She raised her chin and dusted off her hands brusquely. Nonsense. Everything was in order and perfectly sensible. And that's the way she liked things—ordered and controlled. Not like her heartbeat, which was still hammering from the look in Grady's intense blue eyes.

# Chapter Seven

❧

Jennie stared at herself in the mirror. It was like seeing an alien in the place where she used to be. Her jeans weren't designer ones, her shirt was a smaller version of Grady's blue chambray, and her shoes were plain white tennis sneakers instead of her high-heeled designer sandals. Even her hair looked different, tied back with a red-and-white bandanna instead of her usual ribbon. Looking down at herself, she thought she looked ridiculous, but these were the clothes Grady had insisted were necessary, so she supposed she'd better comply.

Taking a final look in the mirror, she swung her pocketbook over her shoulder and went out to her car. It would take a little under half an hour to get to the schoolhouse. It wasn't six-thirty yet, but the sun was already high on the eastern horizon.

When she pulled her car into the driveway, Grady's dilapidated truck was already there. She cut the engine and got out of the car to find him. The sound of lumber being dropped in the schoolhouse told her where he was.

Jennie mounted the sagging front stoop and poked

her head inside. The place already looked like a carpenter's workroom; sawhorses and toolboxes, drop cloths and ladders, power tools and extension cords were all lined up neatly. Grady was bending over a toolbox, an abstracted look on his face.

"Good morning," she called to him. "This place looks like you've set up for the next year."

He grinned at her and stood up. "Unfortunately, I'll have to lug my tools back and forth every weekend because of the other jobs during the week, but I've got everything down to a science, so it won't be too bad."

"Well, one thing can be said for you—you're neat."

"A carpenter has to be, any workman does. Otherwise you'd lose your tools every time you put them down."

Jennie ran her eyes over the conglomeration of tools. "You mean there's a specific place for every tool?"

"There sure is. That way I can find what I need when I need it. I always know where it is."

"Unless you forget to put it back in the same place."

He grinned at her. "No way, Jennie Winters. I *always* put a tool back where it belongs. That's my first rule."

"Then maybe you'd better tell me where everything goes, or I might mess you up."

"Oh, no," he said, shaking his head, his eyes gleaming with humor. "You're not touching my tools—that's my second rule."

"But . . ." Jennie's eyes swiveled to meet his. "How am I going to help you if I don't use your tools?"

His eyes wandered down her body. "Right about now, I'm thinking that you'd be a better help if you kept out of sight. You're quite a distraction as you are."

Jennie's eyes bounced off his as color flooded her

cheeks. She was suddenly aware of his massive shoulders and the hair that rose like a cloud from his chest. His shirt was buttoned only partway and his sleeves were rolled up to reveal his tanned forearms. If he wanted to talk about distractions, then he wasn't going to be easy to work with either.

Jennie looked down at herself and made a comical grimace. "That's funny, I was thinking that I looked like a man in this getup."

Grady's warm blue eyes gleamed. "Oh, no, Ms. Winters. Take it from me, you don't look anything like a man." His eyes ran down her figure and back up again. "Not in the least."

But then he turned away and picked up a small metal tool. "We might as well have a few preparatory lessons," he said, turning back to her. "Today, when I've taken down the trim around the windows and doors, I'll begin punching holes in the plaster ceilings and walls." He held up the metal piece. "This is a utility bar. I'll use it to pry the trim away from the walls, and I'll also use it with a hammer to knock holes in the plaster."

Jennie nodded. "A utility bar."

"Right." He set it down and picked up a heavier, longer piece of metal with a curved end. He hefted it in his hands. "And this is a wrecking bar. I might use it to punch holes in the plaster as well."

"That makes sense—you use a wrecking bar to wreck things."

He nodded. "As I said, I'll be taking down the wood trim first. That will keep me busy for about an hour, I'd say."

"What about me? What do I do?"

He stood looking at the wrecking bar, then looked up at her. "Have you ever used a hammer?"

Jennie threw him a disgusted look. "Of course I've used a hammer!"

He grinned at her. "Sorry if I offended your sensibilities, but you don't look like you're the kind of woman who goes around using hammers and saws and the like."

"I didn't say I'd used a *saw*," she qualified huffily. "But I sure know what to do with a hammer."

"Well, then, you can pull the nails out of the trim that I take down from the windows and doors. If we can, we'll reuse it all, so try to be careful when you're pulling the nails. If you split the wood, it can't be reused."

"Why are you taking the trim down in the first place?"

"Because this old plaster on the walls and ceiling is coming down in places and we have to take it all down to put up drywall. We can't take the plaster down unless we remove the trim." Then he smiled at her. "Well, we *could*, but it would wreck the wood trim along with the plaster, and the first rule on a restoration project is to save as much as you can. It's not only financially advisable, but it's historically accurate. When the room is finished, it will look a lot nicer if we've used some of the old wood."

"Well, that sounds easy enough."

Grady's smile grew. "That is the easy part. Wait until I begin poking holes in the plaster—you'll wish you were a million miles away."

"Why's that?"

"It's dirty work. There'll be plaster dust all over the place, and you'll be the one who has to cart it out to my truck."

"Oh." She stared at the walls and ceiling, not convinced that she would wish she was a million miles away. This was going to be her home, after all, so she wanted to be in on everything. And this was all proving to be very exciting, very exciting indeed.

Two hours later Jennie wondered if she knew what she was doing to herself. Grady had finished prying off the trim from around the windows and doors in the schoolroom, and he had begun to poke holes into the plaster ceiling. He stood on wood scaffolding and hammered the utility bar into the ceiling, prying out huge chunks of the plaster, which he dropped to the floor. Dust whirled everywhere, and he and Jennie were already covered in it. Jennie's muscles were beginning to protest as she bent to pick up the heavy chunks and lugged them out to the back of his truck.

Grady wore a dust mask and had offered to let Jennie have one, but she'd refused. Now, as she coughed and wiped her sleeve across her nose, she wished she hadn't been so ready to refuse something Grady offered her.

Up on the scaffolding, Grady paused in his work and looked down at her. "Want a dust mask yet?" he asked as if he were making polite conversation.

Jennie's eyes skittered away from his. "Well, I suppose it wouldn't hurt."

She knew he was grinning because it was written all over his face, what she could see of it around the mask. She reached up and quickly took the mask from his hands, then fastened it across her nose and mouth, feeling belligerence well up inside her. Damn the man anyway! Why did he have to act like she was a little tenderfoot? Granted, she might not know what she was doing, but she was willing, wasn't she?

She bent to pick up a huge piece of plaster, and then she lifted it and for what seemed the hundredth time began the trek to the back of his truck. By noon her muscles were screaming in protest. When Grady stopped, declaring it was time for lunch, she fell into step beside him, and they went outside to sit under one of the maples in the front yard.

Flopping down on the grass, Jennie took a deep breath and let it out slowly. She felt as if she had been lugging plaster all her life, and she was getting nowhere with the work. There were still huge piles of it sitting on the floor; Grady was working faster than she could keep up with him.

She lay back on the grass and closed her eyes, then opened them at the sound of paper rustling. Turning her head, she saw that Grady was unwrapping a huge sandwich. The sight of it made her mouth water, and she sat up, aghast.

"Lunch!" she cried. "I forgot! I don't have anything to eat!"

Without a word, Grady reached into his black lunch pail and handed her another sandwich.

"Oh, but I couldn't . . ." Her mouth watered as she stared at it.

"Why not?"

"It's yours."

He shook his head and indicated the lunch pail. "I have two more. I figured you'd forget."

With a quiet thank-you, she took the sandwich and began unwrapping it. Somehow she felt like a child and Grady was her teacher, tolerant of her foibles but beginning to tire rapidly. She stared down at the huge sandwich and bit into it, looking up to find Grady holding out a mug of thick, dark coffee.

"Here," he said. "Drink up. You'll need it. That's tiring work you're doing."

She took the mug from his hands and drank greedily, wincing at the taste. "What'd you do?" she asked after she coughed and spluttered. "Make it from old shoes?"

He grinned his slow, easy grin. "Nope. I just like good strong coffee."

"Strong, all right, but that coffee's liable to get up and walk away."

Grady's eyes took on a humorous gleam. "Maybe we could get it to tote some of that plaster. You look like you could use some help."

She lifted her chin haughtily. "I'm doing all right. I haven't called for any help yet, have I?"

"Not yet, but then that could be because you're half-strangled by the plaster dust. If I'm working you too hard, just speak up, Jennie."

Mutely she shook her head. She was damned if she'd ask him for help. She had told him she'd help, and she meant to. She wasn't about to turn into a pussyfoot, crying out for help.

But before he went back to work, Grady walked over to his truck and got in. "I'm going to back this up to one of the windows. There's no sense you toting that heavy stuff all the way out to the driveway."

Jennis said nothing, just stood and watched as he backed the half-filled truck up to a window and then got out.

"How's that?" he asked. "That should make it easier for you."

Her chin rose a quarter of an inch. "You didn't have

to do that for me, you know. I'm capable of lugging that plaster out to the truck."

He reached out and flicked a finger under her chin. "I know you are, McGee," he said softly. "I'm just trying to help you out, that's all."

"Who's McGee?" she asked belligerently, shaking her chin from his grasp.

He grinned at her. "You are, but I'll call you Winters if you insist."

"Why not just call me Jennie?"

His blue eyes gleamed at her. "It's too personal, and you do want me to keep my distance, right?"

Pink color flooded her cheeks as her eyes skittered away from his. "Oh. Yes, er . . . that's right . . ." She paused, then felt her lips curving into a smile. "O'Hara."

He grinned back at her, then turned away and mounted the scaffold to begin chipping holes into the plaster and letting it drop to the floor once again.

Their weekends fell into a similar pattern. Grady told Jennie what to do, and she did it, slowly at first, then with more confidence. After the first weekend, her muscles screamed in protest and she was sore for the following week, but she gradually got used to the physical exercise and she began to blossom. Her excitement at seeing the schoolhouse progress was contagious. Grady began to catch it, and she found herself wishing he hadn't; he began whistling tunelessly, and it set her teeth on edge.

Two weeks after she had begun working with him, they began insulating the outer walls. They had stripped the plaster and Grady had carted it off to the dump. When the outer walls' framework was exposed, Grady showed her how to measure and cut the insulation bats and left her to her chore, while he began building the framework for the bathroom and kitchen walls, after he'd torn out the old cloakroom walls.

Jennie was on her hands and knees cutting the insulation bats, and Grady was whistling as he measured a board for the bathroom wall framing.

"Grady!" she finally exclaimed. "Can't you whistle a *tune*, for crying out loud?"

"This is a tune," he said, turning to her. "What's wrong with it?"

"What's *wrong* with it?" she exclaimed. "It raises the hair on the back of my neck, that's what's wrong with it!"

He grinned his infuriating grin. "Well, I'm sorry, mademoiselle. I wasn't aware that you were a music critic."

"Anybody'd be a music critic where *that* squawk was concerned!" But she found herself beginning to grin back at him. "Oh . . . all right. Go ahead. Whistle. But stop every five minutes or so and give my poor ears a rest, will you?"

"I'll do better than that. I'll bring in a radio. Would that suit your patrician ears better?"

"It depends what you play on it. Country-and-western I can do without."

"How about hard rock?"

She made a back-and-forth motion with her hand. "So-so."

"Then we'll settle for easy listening. How's that?"

She smiled at him, sitting back on her heels. "That's fine."

"Good. Anything else I can do for you?"

She screwed up her face in an exaggerated motion

and seemed to ponder his question. "Well, now that you mention it, I'm getting sick and tired of roast-beaf sandwiches every weekend. How about peanut butter and jelly once in a while? Can you make those?"

He put down his tape measure and walked toward her. "I can make anything your heart desires. Ham and cheese, chicken salad, pastrami on rye, bologna, or salami. I also do a mean brunch. Care to come over to my house next Sunday and sample my eggs Benedict?"

"Eggs Benedict? You *are* a gourmet!"

"I can also do a great Vermont Hardy. That's a pile of flapjacks with sausage and bacon, all smothered in melted butter and hot syrup, fresh from Vermont, blueberry muffins on the side."

"Ohhh," she groaned in ecstasy. "Do you know what I had to eat this morning, Grady? One measly English muffin, in the motel coffee shop."

"Then it's settled. Next Sunday you come to my place before we start work and I'll make my famous country brunch."

She found herself smiling at him. "And what's the famous country brunch?"

"It's a Vermont Hardy combined with scrambled eggs and Canadian bacon. Think you'll like it?"

"I'll love it. Say no more, I'm famished already."

He glanced at his watch. "It's almost time to quit for lunch now, anyway."

She scrambled up from the floor and followed him outside to sit in the shade. When they had settled down and begun eating, Jennie glanced toward him.

"Have you been doing this work long, Grady?"

"I began when I was a kid, working summers with an old Swedish carpenter in my hometown in Massachusetts.

He's the one who taught me about carpentry, and he really loved old buildings. He passed that on to me, too." He paused and poured a mug of his strong coffee. "When I went away to college, I became a history major, and I often think it was because of old Gus. His love of old things really rubbed off on me."

"You went to college?" Jennie found herself staring at him, surprised at this unexpected news.

"Does it surprise you?" he asked.

Color flared in her cheeks. "Well . . . you're a carpenter, Grady. How many carpenters go to school?"

"Do you always jump to conclusions, Jennie Winters?" he asked softly.

She felt the fire in her cheeks burning from the censure in his eyes. "I guess I did jump to a conclusion. I'm sorry."

He waved away her apology. "It doesn't matter. I found out a long time ago that it doesn't matter what people think. The only thing that matters is what I think."

Jennie smiled, recalling Gladys Peevy's words that Grady was his own man. "Were you always this independent, Mr. O'Hara?" she asked teasingly. "Or is it something new?"

He shook his head. "No, there was a time when I lived a pretty conventional life, Jennie. I had what most people thought was a good job. I had a nice home, a wife—everything that a man is supposed to want."

"A wife?" She found herself staring at him again. "You were married?"

He nodded. "For about four years. Then we split up. Laura and I wanted different things out of life, but I only found that out after we'd been married awhile."

"Different things?"

He nodded. "Yes, Laura wanted money and prestige and social standing. I was working as a curator in a museum, and it wasn't enough for her. She'd have liked me to be the director of the museum. She was like a leach, living off me, wanting to get her prestige from her husband's job.

"And all the time, all I wanted to do was work with old buildings. I got to hate my life. It was a continual round of cocktail parties and meetings and three-piece suits. Finally, Laura left me. She ended up in Wellesley, near Boston. She's married to a banker now and has two kids and attends teas and society luncheons and she's happy as a clam.

"As for me, I got a job at Sturbridge Village for a couple of years, then started my own business. At first it was scary, but then I began getting contracts and I knew I'd make it."

"And . . ." Jennie hesitated. "You don't miss your wife?"

"No, that was a long time ago, Jennie. Over eight years. I'd married her when I was still in college, when I was still a boy. I stopped loving her a long time ago."

"But now—is this enough for you? Your work? Is that enough, Grady?"

"For now it is. I don't have time to be lonely, Jennie. I work long days, all over New England. I'm getting a reputation for myself, and it's surprising how busy I am."

"My work had always been enough for me, too—until lately. I got promoted to officer last year after eleven years of hard work, and suddenly the bottom seemed to drop out of my world. I'd gotten what I'd worked so hard for, and suddenly it wasn't enough. That's when I decided to look for a weekend place. When I saw the schoolhouse . . ." She looked over at Grady and smiled. "Well, now I'm happy again. Busy, but happy."

"And what about you—have you ever been married?" Grady asked.

Jennie shook her head as she munched on her sandwich. "No, not even tempted. I've been too busy working, I guess."

"Do you have family around here?"

"My parents live in West Hartford and I have a younger sister who's married and has two kids. They live in Simsbury."

Grady sat back against the maple tree and smiled at her. "Tell me about them. About yourself."

Jennie smiled and took another bite from her sandwich. "There's not much to tell, Grady. We're a *very* conventional family. Dad works for Reliable Insurance and Mother . . ." Jennie paused, then went on slowly. "Mother sounds a lot like your ex-wife, Laura. Mother is big on clubs. She belongs to so many I can't keep them straight. She's always going on about some society ball or charity luncheon." Jennie grinned ruefully. "Sometimes I think she's the reason I became such an avid career woman. My mother's life is so *useless*."

"Sounds like you're the family rebel."

Jennie shook her head. "Oh, no. If I rebel, it's generally in a socially acceptable way. I'm pretty conventional too, Grady."

He stretched out on the grass and put his arms under his head, his eyes watching her. "I think I knew that already, Ms. Winters. The first time we met, you gave ample evidence of being shocked at your own behavior."

Jennie felt her cheeks drain of all color. Aghast, she stared at the rest of her sandwich and she knew she wouldn't be able to finish it. She had dreaded this moment, dreaded the time that Grady would bring up what had happened on that first day. She'd tried to blot it out of her mind, but now it was back again, staring her in the face, and she didn't know what to say. Apprehensively she glanced at Grady and saw that he was grinning at her. Color immediately rushed back into her face, heating her cheeks.

"Hey," he said softly, sitting up and reaching out to smooth a piece of her hair back from her face. "Don't look like that, Jennie. It wasn't such a horrible thing to happen."

Against her will, she felt her eyes lifting to his. It was as if she were powerless against his magnetism. She sat on the grass and felt the breeze gently brush her hair back, but the feel of his touch still lingered on her cheek. Jennie was still so conscious of it that she raised her hand and pressed it to her face, still mesmerized by those incredibly blue eyes.

"Do you know that you have gold flecks in your eyes?" he whispered, searching her eyes with his.

She nodded mutely, her hand still resting lightly on her cheek, unable to break the spell he had woven. She felt as if she were drowning in his eyes, being drawn into them as a swimmer is pulled by an undertow. She felt her breath stop, then her heartbeat begin to accelerate. She knew that he was going to kiss her, knew that she wanted him to, and she was powerless to resist.

Jennie watched, enthralled, as his head came down to hers. Without volition, her own lifted and then her eyes were closing and she was being drawn into his strong arms. It felt as if she were being enclosed in warm steel. The heat from his body enveloped her as he held her against his rock-hard body and their lips touched. With that touch all feeling exploded in myriad sensations. Jennie's arms stole around his body and she knew she was clinging to him, knew that her lips were parting to admit his tongue, and then there was no more thought. Suddenly everything was feeling—a golden rush of pleasure that filled her as his tongue entwined with hers. She felt the velvety glide of it against her own, and the shock of it coursed through her body. Wave after wave of pleasure welled up in her, and Jennie felt herself being transported into ecstasy.

Then the kiss was ending. She stared into Grady's eyes and felt her world careening out of control.

"You see?" he murmured. "It's not so bad, is it?"

# Chapter Eight

Jennie felt her lips curve into a smile as she gazed into his warm blue eyes. "Not bad at all," she murmured.

"But it's time to get back to work," he said, grinning lopsidedly. "And for the first time in memory, I wish it weren't."

"You love your work, don't you, Grady?"

He took a deep breath and turned his head to gaze at the tree across the road. "Nothing means as much to me as working with wood, Jennie. I love the feel of it under my hand. I love the smell of it when I'm working with it. That's why I felt like such a misfit when I worked at the museum. I was like a fish out of water."

Jennie watched him carefully, suddenly realizing that she was as interested in what he had to say as she was in his incredible good looks. "Don't you miss the prestige of your job at the museum?"

"Prestige?" he asked, grinning at her. "What do I need with prestige? I'm happy doing what I'm doing, Jennie, and I have a feeling there are an awful lot of men, and probably women too who are tied to jobs they hate just because they don't have the courage to leave them.

"After Laura left me, it seemed there wasn't anything to live for, and that's when I made the break and finally did what I wanted to do. I thought that by working at Sturbridge Village I'd meet my needs, but even that didn't completely satisfy me. Nothing works for me but to actually get my hands dirty working with old buildings. So I bit the bullet and started my construction business. I'd bought the saltbox and was fixing it up, and I never seemed to have enough money, but slowly the work started coming my way, and now I wouldn't change it for the world. I'm happy, Jennie—as happy as a man has a right to be. I wouldn't change anything . . ." He hesitated, glancing at her. "Well, maybe one or two things."

She smiled at him. "Like what?"

"Well, I guess my life could stand having a woman in it."

Her eyes sparkled at him. "But I thought you said a while ago that you didn't have time to be lonely. So you do miss your wife, after all."

"No, I didn't say that. I said I could stand having a woman in my life again. I didn't say I wanted the woman to be Laura. Laura wasn't right for me, but I didn't realize that until too late."

"But you said that you felt like there wasn't anything left to live for when she left you."

"That's how I felt then, more than eight years ago. It was hard having her walk out on me. She'd been telling me that I wasn't ambitious enough, and that's hard on a man. It wasn't until she left and I was at Sturbridge Village that I realized that I *was* ambitious, but not in the way she wanted me to be."

Jennie looked at him curiously. "In what way, then?"

"I have plans for myself. I don't intend to be just a local carpenter forever. I want to be known as the best restoration man in New England. That means a lot of hard work in the next few years, but I'm ready for it."

"How do you go about becoming the best, Grady?"

"By getting as many jobs with old buildings as I can. That way I'll become as knowledgeable as I can and develop my carpentry and restoration skills." He paused and grinned at her. "And a little luck wouldn't hurt."

She found herself excited for him, with as much interest in his subject as he seemed to feel. It surprised Jennie for she'd never thought that construction work could be interesting to her. But then she realized that Grady himself was interesting, so naturally what he did was interesting.

And, incredibly, she had just kissed this man, had experienced the heart-stopping wonder of it, and yet she was still able to sit and talk with him as if nothing had happened. What other man could move her physically the way Grady did, then just as easily engage her intellect?

Jennie stood up and looked at the trees across the road, trying to find an answer, but there wasn't one. Grady O'Hara was special, but what kind of future could she have with him? Unable to answer her own questions, she turned and went back into the schoolhouse. Grady trailed after her, and for the rest of the afternoon they worked quietly on the insulation. Jennie didn't want to talk, there were too many questions in her mind, and she felt a desperate need to sort them all out.

On Monday morning Jennie sailed into her office and found the usual stack of mail awaiting her. She deposited her pocketbook in her desk drawer, leaned down to

smell her African violets, then settled behind the metal
desk in her utilitarian orange tweed chair to sort out the
mail. She tossed two circulars into the wastebasket,
opened a large manila interoffice envelope and took out
the memo, read it swiftly, and filed it for her secretary to
handle. A small square envelope caught her eye, and she
frowned as she tried to remember where she'd seen the
handwriting before. Then her face cleared as she recognized Martha Powell's handwriting. Martha was married to
her boss, John Powell, and every year about this time
Jennie received an invitation to their annual cocktail party.
Slitting open the envelope, she drew out the invitation,
then glanced at her calendar. The cocktail party was a
month away. Jennie had gone for ten consecutive years
now, and she idly wondered whom she would invite
to go with her. Grady's image floated before her.

Startled, she crammed the invitation back into its envelope and tried to push the thought of Grady from her
mind. What was she thinking of? Grady O'Hara was
simply the carpenter she'd hired to renovate the schoolhouse. It was nonsense to think of inviting him to attend
the Powells' exclusive cocktail party with her. If she
were going to invite someone, Dana Avery was a more
likely candidate. He looked like all the other men who
attended—slightly preppy, with the right clothes and
social connections. Grady just wouldn't fit in. It was silly
to think he would.

But as the week progressed, Jennie found herself
repeatedly thinking of Grady. At odd moments, while
dictating a letter or trying to write a report, she would
remember his kiss and all the ecstasy that went with it.
Her heartbeat would accelerate as she once again experienced the sensations of being kissed by Grady O'Hara.

Astounded at herself and her reactions, Jennie tried to shake herself back into reality again and again. She had a dozen things to do, and sitting at her desk mooning over a man wasn't one of them. In her twelve years at TransContinental, this had never happened before. She had always been able to neatly compartmentalize her life, separating men from her job. But, then again, she had always dated dull and uninteresting men. Now she realized she had been kissed and made love to by a man who had the power to move her to the heights of rapture. It was no small wonder that he invaded her thoughts at work.

She stared at her surroundings, the beige desk, the filing cabinets, and the metal bookcases crammed with insurance tomes, in an effort to get Grady out of her thoughts and reassure herself that this was all that mattered. For twelve years she had been devoted to her work, and now she had suddenly come smack up against the hardest question of her career: was work the only thing she wanted in her life? Had she been truthful when she told Grady that since buying the schoolhouse she had everything she wanted? Did she need more? Her body's traitorous response to Grady's lovemaking seemed to indicate that she did.

But did she want a man who was so different from her? Asking herself that, Jennie had to chuckle at the irony of life. Two months ago, when she first met Dana Avery, she had complained that all the men in her life were made from the same mold. Now she had finally met a man distinctly different from any other, yet she was still hesitating, unsure about becoming involved with *him*.

The questions haunted Jennie the rest of the week,

and by Friday she'd had enough. Exasperated, she decided she'd do something about it. When she drove out to Stockton that afternoon, she stopped by Dana Avery's home. By the time she got there, the shadows were stretching across the road. She didn't know why she had come here, but she knew that Dana Avery was what she needed—a reassuring man whom she could handle.

She found him on the back terrace with his daughter, Lucy, and a boy who looked to be his son, Danny.

"Jennie Winters!" He stood up and held out his hand, looking genuinely pleased to see her.

"Dana, I thought it was about time I got to know my neighbors in Stockton, so here I am."

"And not a minute too soon. Lucy and Danny are going to play tennis, leaving me to my own devices. Now I don't have to worry. You can entertain me."

She laughed and let him pour her a glass of lemonade. "Sure you won't take something stronger?" he asked.

"This is fine. I'm a lemonade freak."

When they settled in the lawn chairs, he smiled at her. "What brings you into town? Isn't Grady keeping you busy enough?"

She gave a playful grimace. "He's a regular slave driver. My muscles will never be the same."

"Then I can't interest you in a doubles match with Danny and Lucy?"

Jennie shook her head, turning toward the small boy who sat on the far side of the terrace. "This must be Danny."

Dana nodded. "Danny, this is Jennie Winters. She bought the schoolhouse you love so much."

The boy turned his head and looked at Jennie curiously. "Are you really going to live there? All the time?"

"Well, just on weekends for starters," Jennie said. "Maybe someday I'll move in for good, but for now it's just a weekend home."

"And you're working on it, too? With Grady?" Danny asked eagerly.

Jennie laughed. "Let's just say I'm helping Grady out. Sometimes, though, it seems like I'm more of a hindrance."

"I worked with Grady once. Remember, Dad? It was before Mom went away."

"Yes, son, I remember. Why don't you and Lucy go on and play that tennis match?"

The boy made a face, which was echoed by his sister; then both got up and walked toward the tennis court.

"They're nice kids, Dana."

"Yes, they are." He heaved a sigh and took a long sip of lemonade. "Sometimes I wonder how I'm doing with them, though. It's been rough since Eleanor left."

"Eleanor was your wife?"

He nodded, his eyes on his children's retreating backs. "Yes, she left me, you know. It's been about four years now, but sometimes it feels like fourteen."

Jennie watched him with sympathetic eyes. "Have you thought of remarrying? Getting a new mother for the kids?"

"Oh, yes, I've thought of it, but it isn't all that easy to find the right woman, especially when she realizes she'll be taking on a ready-made family." He glanced at her and grinned. "How about you? Would you be willing?"

Jennie laughed softly. "They're lovely kids, I'd almost be tempted."

Dana looked at her with speculative eyes. "What would stop you?"

She grinned easily. "I haven't the requisite experience. I should think you'd want someone who's done a little mothering on her own already."

"Not necessarily. You could learn."

She shook her head, smiling. "If this is a proposal, Mr. Avery, it's coming too fast for me. Slow down, will you?"

He grinned back at her and took another swig of his lemonade. "You'll stay for supper, won't you? The kids would love it, and so would I. We're having chicken on the grill."

"Sounds wonderful. I'd love it."

The rest of the afternoon passed in easy banter accompanied by the laughter and shrill cries from the tennis court. Then the the children ran back from the court and pandemonium ensued as Dana started the coals and they clustered around, including Jennie in their fun. Dinner was served on the terrace. Grilled chicken, corn on the cob, tossed salad, and hot rolls all served on a picnic table where they sat and ate, laughing and joking their way through the meal. Then Lucy and Danny were sent off to bed and Dana lit citronella candles against the mosquitoes. Jennie and he swung together on the porch swing.

"This has been fun, Dana," Jennie said after they had sat for a while without speaking. "You have a lovely old home."

"I'm glad you like it. It was Eleanor's pride and joy. Sometimes I think it's all that kept her here for the last years of our marriage."

Jennie made a comforting sound, but Dana waved it aside. "No, I mean it, Jennie. This house was Eleanor's passion. When I first met her, I brought her home to meet my father and she fell in love with the house. It was falling down and in terrible need of repairs when Dad died. We moved here from Boston and Eleanor started researching the history of the house. She spent over a year just going through family correspondence and looking at the old pictures, trying to dig up how the house had looked when it was originally built. After she researched it, she started renovating one room at a time. Of course, the place is huge, there are eighteen rooms, so it took her awhile."

"She did it all on her own?"

"Everything that she could, she did on her own. If she needed an expert, someone to do the plastering or the carpentry, then she'd hire someone, but Eleanor did all of the painting and refinishing and the hand stenciling."

"Is that when Grady worked here? While she was restoring it?"

Dana hesitated; then he spoke slowly. "Grady moved to town about six years ago, just after he left Sturbridge and started his own business. Sometimes I think Eleanor single-handedly got him started in his business. He was here so much during the last two years of our marriage that I was beginning to think he lived here." Dana paused, rocking the porch swing slowly, his eyes unseeing as he looked out toward the tennis courts. "It got to be that Grady and Eleanor were inseparable. I'd never see one without the other. I'd come home from the office and he'd be here and I'd get up to go to work in the morning and he'd be here then."

Jennie turned to look at him, her eyes troubled. "You were pleased with his work, weren't you?"

He didn't answer for a moment. "What?" he asked finally. "Pleased with his work? Oh, sure, of course. His work was first-rate. I wouldn't have recommended him to you if it wasn't. No, I was just remembering, that's all." He heaved a sigh. "Just remembering . . ."

Jennie rocked back and forth at the tempo that Dana set, but she felt unsettled. Somehow, the moment the talk had gotten around to Grady, she had sensed that Dana was holding something back. She couldn't put a finger on what it was that seemed out of place, but she knew that somehow, subtly, the mood had changed.

"Then your wife left, is that right?" she prompted gently.

"What? Oh, yes. Eleanor left about four years ago, right after the house was finished. I joked with Grady once that he shouldn't have worked so fast—maybe Eleanor would have stayed if there was more work to be done." He forced a chuckle. "You couldn't keep Eleanor away from Gra . . ." He stopped abruptly and cleared his throat. "You couldn't keep her away from restoration work. She loved it. Loved everything about it."

But Jennie had stopped listening. Suddenly she knew what bothered her about the conversation. Somehow, in some small way, she had gotten the impression that Eleanor Avery had been interested in Grady in more than a professional way. What had Dana been about to say? That he couldn't keep his wife away from Grady? If so, did it mean that Grady O'Hara was involved in the breakup of Eleanor and Dana Avery's marriage?

Jennie was deep in thought when she suddenly realized that Dana had stopped talking and had put his arm around her. The warmth might have been welcome, but somehow Jennie didn't relish the idea of fending off Dana's advances. Cursing herself inwardly, she realized too late that while she might have welcomed Dana's easy companionship, she wouldn't welcome his kisses or caresses. After kissing Grady O'Hara, there could be nothing for her from a man like Dana. But how could she tactfully let him know that?

She was about to turn her head to say something light and innocuous when Dana's head came down and he was kissing her. Startled, Jennie let him kiss her, then broke away.

"I've got to be going now, Dana. Supper was wonderful and I really enjoyed talking with the kids, but I really have to go now."

"Don't go," he said, taking her in his arms. "Stay with me, Jennie. Stay all night."

"Dana, please . . ."

"I know," he said wearily. "I talked too much about Eleanor, didn't I?"

"No, of course not. I enjoyed hearing about her. You make her sound fascinating."

"That's just the trouble. She is. Totally and unremittingly fascinating. Even when I'm with an attractive woman, I can't get her out of my head."

"She must be very beautiful," Jennie said softly.

"Oh, God, she is! As beautiful a creature as you'd ever want to see. Hair like an angel's . . ." He broke off and smothered a curse, then grabbed for Jennie and brought his lips down crushingly on hers. He groaned when Jennie fought him. "Kiss me, dammit! Help me banish her!"

Jennie pushed him back and stood up. "Dana, this isn't the way to forget your wife! Find a woman who's as enticing to you as she is and you'll forget her automatically. You can't do it by trying to take any woman that happens along."

"But you're beautiful, dammit! I find you enticing."

"Nonsense. You find me attractive, but you're still half in love with your wife." Jennie smiled sadly. "Maybe even three-quarters in love with her." Jennie put her hand out and touched his shoulder. "Give yourself time, Dana. Don't rush things."

"Rush things?" he echoed incredulously. "My God, she's been gone four years now. Who's trying to *rush* things? You'd think by now my life would have gotten back to normal."

Jennie sat down on the edge of the swing. "What happened, Dana? Why did she leave?"

He shook his head. "I don't know. I've never really known. I don't know if it was me or this town. She got to hate Stockton. She called it a one-horse town. She was from Boston, you know, and she liked Stockton well enough in the beginning. It was kind of a novelty to her, I think. She pretended she was the lady of the manor and all that, lording it over everyone. But as the house progressed, she got bored and she took to drinking too much, holding wild parties for all her friends from Boston." He laughed sourly. "Lord, she was the bane of Stockton's existence. One night she held a party for all her society friends and they all got absolutely wiped out; then they piled into Eleanor's sports car and went careening all over town. Eleanor was driving, and on a lark she went down the side of the green and ran over everyone's mailboxes. Lord, what a racket! You could hear them all over town."

Dana grimaced as he recalled the story. "Well, when the constable realized it was her and he got very apologetic, but he still brought her into police headquarters and called me to come get her. By the time I got there,

Eleanor was having a field day with him—making fun of him and what she called his *bucolic* ways." Dana put his head to his hand. "God, it was horrible! I was mortified, yet at the same time I was oddly excited by it all. She was like a dazzling princess gracing this lowly town and paying us all an enormous compliment by being here."

"But surely you didn't feel *beneath* her?"

He smiled sadly. "Yes, I think in a way I did. Oh, I've got the money and the old family and the looks, but Eleanor was *real* class, Jennie. She radiated money and prestige and social standing. She was the most exciting woman I've ever known. I think that any man who ever knew her would feel that way. There was a kind of mystique about her, a radiance . . ." He trailed off and sat looking toward the tennis courts. "She's the one who had those tennis courts built. 'Put them in the backyard, darling' she said to me. 'We'll be the only ones in this one-horse town to have our own courts.' " Dana smiled. "And so I did. Anything she asked for, I gave her. I spoiled her unmercifully. I don't even give the kids half of what I gave her."

Jennie sat in silence for a while; then she stood up. "Dana, I really do have to go. . . ."

He looked up at her and seemed astonished that she was there, as if he had been talking to himself. "God, I wish you wouldn't. You're helping me more than you know. This is the first time I've really been able to talk about her in four years."

"Then perhaps it's what you need," Jennie said gently. "Perhaps now you'll be able to forget her."

"Then stay awhile, Jennie. Stay with me and help me banish her completely."

She shook her head, but smiled to soften her refusal.

"I can't, Dana. I've got to be out to the schoolhouse by seven tomorrow."

"Ah, yes, Grady," Dana said bitterly. "The taskmaster. I remember he used to be here at seven every morning and Eleanor was always there beside him. You couldn't keep her away from him. She worshiped him, I think. Him and his damn knowledge of old buildings."

Troubled, Jennie stared down at Dana. "She worshiped Grady? In . . . in what way, Dana?"

He waved his hand in irritation. "How the hell should I know? I was only her poor blighted husband. She never confided in me."

"But you suspect something, don't you, Dana?"

"Suspect something?" he cried. "No, there's nothing to suspect. Oh, I imagine she wanted Grady, but he wouldn't have her, Jennie. He worked with her all day long and didn't even give a fig for her. That's what amazes me about the man. How could he work alongside her for two years and not be crazy about her? But he wasn't, not Grady O'Hara." He chuckled bitterly. "And she wanted him. I saw that she did, but he wouldn't have her. Sometimes I think that's why she went away. Not because of me, not because the restoration was finished, but because that damned carpenter wouldn't have her. The only man in her life, I think, who ever refused her. Yes," said Dana, nodding his head slowly. "The only one who never wanted her."

# Chapter Nine

The next morning, Grady began installing the wallboard on the ceilings. Jennie had to stand on the wooden scaffolding next to him and hold up the heavy four-by-eight sheets while he hammered the nails into place. It was hard and awkward work and it made conversation difficult, but Jennie was thankful for that. She had too much to think about to want to talk to Grady, and he seemed too immersed in his work to want to talk.

As she stood next to him on the scaffolding, she remembered what Dana Avery had said about Grady and Eleanor Avery. It didn't come as a surprise that Eleanor had been attracted to Grady; Jennie realized from her own feelings that most women would find him desirable. What she found peculiarly fascinating was the fact that Grady had worked alongside a notoriously beautiful woman and hadn't succumbed to her, yet he had made love to Jennie within minutes of meeting her.

Thinking about this as she helped him, Jennie wondered if Dana Avery knew the entire story. Did he hide from the truth to spare his own feelings? Had Grady actually had an affair with Eleanor Avery? Was he part of the reason she left Stockton?

Working alongside him, Jennie couldn't believe Grady was capable of conducting an affair with a married woman, and Dana had said that there had been no attraction on Grady's part, but some small part of Jennie refused to believe in him totally. A nagging doubt remained, and as long as it did, she didn't think she'd be able to trust Grady completely.

Late that afternoon, when it was time to quit for the day, Grady mentioned brunch the next day.

"You're coming, aren't you?" he asked as he walked her to her car.

"Oh . . ." She hesitated, not knowing what to say. "I guess I'd forgotten—or not taken you seriously."

"I was entirely serious, Jennie. I'd like you to come by for brunch. I've gone out and bought all the food and I've even cleaned house for the occasion."

"Well, then, how can I refuse?" she found herself smiling up at him, devastatingly aware of his height and broad shoulders. When she wore these flat sneakers, he towered over her, making her even more conscious of his potent masculinity.

"Then you can sleep late tomorrow. No need to get here at seven o'clock."

"What time shall I come to your place?"

"Oh, say, about ten. How's that?"

She smiled up at him. "It's wonderful. I haven't slept late on a weekend since we've started on this job. Can I bring something, Grady?"

"Not a thing. Just yourself. After we finish, we can still get in a few good hours of work over here."

Jennie groaned playfully. "You *are* a hard taskmaster, Mr. O'Hara."

"But I'm a dynamite cook," he said, grinning at her. "See you tomorrow morning."

She nodded, then stood and watched him drive away in his dilapidated truck. As she got into her own car, she wondered what tomorrow might bring.

Sunday proved to be a perfect day. Jennie pulled back her draperies to find the sky a field of pure blue occasionally broken up by white puffy clouds. The air was clear and dry, an oddity for the end of July in Connecticut. As she drove toward Stockton, she inhaled the fresh country smells and felt peace envelop her.

Pulling into Grady's driveway, she was reminded of that first day she had driven here. She'd expected to meet an old man; then she ran into the dynamo that was Grady O'Hara. As she got out of the car, Kaiser's barking greeted her and the dog ran around from the backyard.

"Hello, Kaiser," she said, leaning down to pat the huge dog. "My God, you're growing!"

Grady's laughter brought her head up. He was dressed in clean jeans and a white button-down shirt with the top button undone and his sleeves rolled up to his elbows. He stood at the corner of the house, his hands on his lean hips.

"Come on, Kaiser. Stop bothering the lady."

Kaiser immediately left Jennie and ran back toward his master, barking delightedly. Jennie followed more slowly, drinking in the beauty of the day. Her eyes fell on the mass of perennial flowers that bloomed along the low rock wall surrounding Grady's property.

"Grady, don't tell me you're a gardener, too," she called out, and began walking toward the perennial border that skirted the driveway.

Grady walked over to join her. "I work on these when I need a break from carpentry. It's a hobby of mine."

Jennie stood and took in the abundant day lilies, helianthus, lythrum, and liatris, the phlox, coreopsis, and oriental poppies. They grew in a bed five feet deep and at least twenty-five feet long, broken only by pockets of annuals, which she suspected would add color when the perennials weren't blooming.

"It's beautiful," she breathed, leaning to inhale the sweet scents. "You're an artist with flowers."

Grady smiled and led her to the back of the red saltbox. There was a fieldstone terrace with redwood furniture on it, and the picnic table was already set up with food and place settings.

Jennie stood and stared at the table, taking in the checked cloth, the white plates, and a massive bouquet of flowers stuck into an old ironstone pitcher. There was a pitcher of Bloody Marys and a platter of small blueberry muffins, cornbread, and sticky buns.

"Grady, you take my breath away," she said as she turned to him after taking it all in. "This is beautiful. I'm completely flabbergasted."

"Well, Jennie, I found out a long time ago that living alone can be pretty bad without a woman to fix things up for me. So I began to watch how women did things and I decided that I'd do for myself and my guests what women usually do. It makes it a heck of a lot nicer than just sitting down to a frozen dinner cooked in an aluminum plate. That's how I lived the first year or so after

Laura left me, and I decided there had to be a better way."

"Well, I think you found it."

He grinned at her and gestured toward the icy pitcher. "Would you like a Bloody Mary? Or would you rather have champagne?"

"Good heavens, no champagne for me. We're going to work this afternoon, aren't we?"

"We sure are. Now that we've got the ceilings done, I want to put up the drywall on the walls. We should make a dent in it this afternoon, and we can finish up next weekend."

He poured a Bloody Mary and handed her the glass, then disappeared into the house to make the scrambled eggs and pancakes. Jennie took a seat in one of the redwood chairs and laid her head back, gazing up through the trees to the dazzling blue sky. As she sipped the drink, she felt peaceful and relaxed as she hadn't in months. Stretching her long legs out in front of her, she closed her eyes and cradled the drink on her stomach as she let her mind wander aimlessly.

The sound of the screen door banging shut brought her eyes open. She looked up to find Grady bearing down on the table with platters of food.

"Come and get it," he called.

She stood up and approached the picnic table. It was groaning with food; heaps of pancakes steamed on a white ironstone platter, scrambled eggs, bacon, sausage, and Canadian bacon were piled on another, and small pitchers of hot maple syrup and bowls of whipped butter completed the repast.

"Oh, Grady, I'll have to go on a diet."

His eyes swept her figure, then met her gaze. "There's

no way that you'll have to go on a diet, Jennie Winters. Dig in."

She took a seat and began filling her plate with food.

"That's what I like to see—a woman with a hearty appetite."

"What do you expect? You sit me in front of a banquet, and I'll take advantage of it."

They laughed and joked for the rest of the meal, then sat and quietly sipped their coffee. Grady sat next to her, his elbow just grazing hers. Jennie was acutely conscious of him. She felt as if the small hairs on her arm were standing on end whenever his arm brushed hers, yet she made no effort to move her arm. She liked being so close to him, liked the fresh scent of his after-shave and the feel of his arm against hers.

"Tell me about yourself, Jennie," he said, his voice low and intimate.

She cocked her head sideways and considered his request. "Well, what can I say? I'm thirty-two and I have an apartment in West Hartford." She grinned at him. "There was hell to pay five years ago when I moved out of my parents' home, even though my place is only across town. My mother was sure I was going to the devil. It took ages for her to calm down and accept that I was a grown adult."

"You would have been how old? Twenty-seven?"

Jennie nodded. "Certainly old enough to live on my own, but Mother was positive I'd get sick or not know how to clean my own place. It was crazy for a time, but after a while she settled down and realized that I really wasn't going to move back home. It's been pretty peaceful for the past four years or so."

"What did your father say?"

"Oh, Dad never says much. He just lets Mother go on and on and quietly tells me to keep the faith." Jennie laughed softly. "I guess he knows it's useless to try to talk some sense into her."

"I imagine you went to college?" Grady asked.

She nodded. "Mount Holyoke. I was a history major, by the way, the same as you. When I graduated I absolutely panicked. I had no idea what I wanted to do with myself. I just knew I didn't want to end up like my mother, sitting home and going to charity meetings and living for my husband."

"Is that why you've never married?"

"No, I've never met anyone who tempted me. That may sound peculiar, but it's true. I've devoted the last twelve years of my life to my job. It's a very exciting job and I've never felt particularly lonely." Jennie considered that, then added, "Well, sometimes I wonder what it would be like to have a home and a family, but no one's come along to sweep me off my feet, so I've been content to stay at my job."

"What does your job entail?"

"Reports, reports, and more reports," she joked, then laughed at the look on his face. "You don't like writing reports?"

"I can't think of anything I'd detest more."

"Oh, it's not so bad, Grady—I'm practically my own boss. I report to a man named John Powell and he's been sort of a mentor to me. He took me under his wing when I first started at TransContinental and he's been my supervisor ever since. Whenever he gets promoted, I do. It's been a very satisfactory relationship."

"But what do you actually do?"

"Well, I started out in underwriting, then I got a

promotion to write training manuals, then I began working with a group of internal consultants who redesign jobs, and now that I'm an officer, I head up my own small staff of five people. I literally go to meetings almost all day, supervise my staff, and write those infernal reports."

"I'd go crazy."

Jennie laughed softly. "You probably would. You love your work too much to like a desk job."

"Well, since we're finished here, how about a tour of my house?" Grady stood up and looked down at her.

She raised her head and was caught again by his power as he towered over her. The soft cloud of hair welled up from his open collar and his muscular chest stretched the fabric of his shirt tautly, calling her eyes to his trim body.

"All right," she said, and felt him take her arm as she stood up. Butterflies invaded her stomach, and she let him guide her toward the back door, all the while vividly conscious of his after-shave and the feel of his warm hand on her arm.

Grady opened the door and guided her into the kitchen. There were gleaming copper pans hanging from a rack above a center island, a fireplace on the far wall, in front of which stood a circular pine table surrounded by four Windsor bow-back chairs. The floor was brick and the cabinets were a mellow pine. There was a large window that looked out over the backyard, but all Jennie could think about was the man who stood so close to her. She looked around the room and murmured something, but her body was reacting in alarming ways to Grady's nearness. It was as if she were two people, one the visitor commenting on his room, the other a vibrant woman ready to spring to life with his slightest gesture.

"There's a dining room next door," Grady said, "and the living room's in front of that."

Jennie nodded, her eyes drinking in the sight of him, hardly conscious of what he was saying as she stared.

"And I sleep right through there," Grady said softly. "On an old daybed in my study."

Jennie nodded dumbly, suddenly tongue-tied. She tried to think of something intelligent to say, but for some reason her mind wasn't working. Everything seemed to fade as she looked into Grady's deep blue eyes. She shakily reached out and put a hand on the back of one of the kitchen chairs to steady herself.

"The study's where I spend most of my time," he was saying. "I have a desk there and keep my books . . ."

She nodded but realized that she wasn't the least interested in where he kept his books. Something strange was happening to her; she could feel her nipples hardening as she stared at Grady, and she knew that she was becoming more and more conscious of him with every passing moment. And he was just as conscious of her. She saw his eyes grow dark as they traveled down toward her breasts and stayed there. Jennie wondered if he could tell what she was going through just by looking at her.

"But I don't suppose a woman would be interested in a man's study," Grady said softly.

"Oh, but I would be," she said, pouncing on any distraction. If she moved, perhaps she would gain control of herself again. She couldn't just stand here and let Grady's magnetism ensnare her.

He took her arm and guided her toward the door of

the study. As he did so, all her feeling became centered on that spot where his hand burned through her sleeve.

He opened the door and let her step into the room, then followed her, keeping his hand on her. The room was large and airy, with windows that overlooked the back and side yards. There was a large rolltop desk in a corner, and a bed that was made up to look like a couch. Jennie stopped short and stared at it.

"That's my bed," Grady said softly, following her gaze. "It doubles as a couch during the day. Would you like to sit down?"

"No! I mean, yes . . . I mean . . ." She bit her lip and stared at the daybed, feeling the color creep into her cheeks. She glanced at him and then looked away quickly. "I guess I don't know what I mean."

"I won't bite," he said, guiding her toward the couch. "Not unless you want me to."

Her eyes bounced off his as she took a seat; then she looked up at him. "So this is where you sleep."

He nodded, and one corner of his mouth quirked up in a half-grin. "And where I don't sleep. Lately I've done more tossing and turning than sleeping, I'm afraid."

"Oh? Why is that?" She felt her cheeks burn at the look in his eyes.

"I've been thinking of you too much. You don't exactly make a man sleepy, you know, Jennie Winters." He sat down next to her and reached out to touch a strand of hair on her shoulder. She felt his fingers and shivered at his touch.

"Don't I?" she murmured breathlessly.

"Uh-huh," he said huskily, letting his fingers trail across her shoulder, then dip under her thick hair to caress the nape of her neck. "You keep me awake far into the night, when I should be sleeping. You don't know how many nights I've lain here wishing you were with me." He lightly kissed the tip of her nose. "And now you are here."

She inhaled unsteadily and raised her head slowly. "Yes," she whispered. "Now I'm here. . . ."

Her eyes met his and she felt the shock of his gaze down to her toes. Grady's eyes were burning like blue flames, looking into hers with a steady intensity that couldn't be ignored. His fingers lifted from her neck and reached out to caress her face, trailing across her cheek to her ear and pausing there. His touch was as light as a breath, yet she was aware of it as if nothing else existed.

They sat and stared into each other's eyes and nothing else did exist. Slowly, inexorably, his head lowered toward her and she found herself lifting hers to meet him. Her lips parted tremulously; his breath felt warm as his lips came down on hers, soft but strong, savoring each moment as if it were a delicate wine.

Trembling, she went into the circle of his arms and felt his grip tighten around her, pressing her against the hard column of his body. His hands moved over her back and shoulders and her own arms tightened around him as she pressed herself against him, glorying in his body.

"Ahhh," he murmured when his lips lifted from hers. "Jennie Winters, you are a beautiful woman."

She lifted her eyes to his and felt her lips curve into a warm smile "And you," she whispered, "are a beautiful man."

He eased her backward into the pillows, his lips trailing from her ear to the corner of her parted lips and hovering there. For a moment everything was suspended as their eyes caught and held.

"God," he groaned huskily. "I want you, Jennie. I want you so badly."

She stared into the stormy caldrons of his eyes and realized that the decision was hers to make. She must either stop here or not stop at all, but she realized that she didn't want to stop. She wanted this man as much as he wanted her; wanted to feel his skin against hers, wanted to touch his hardness, wanted to know that strong, hair-covered chest against her breasts once more. She relaxed into the pillows and let all her desire shine in her eyes.

"And I want you, Grady," she whispered.

His eyes searched hers, blue flames tangling with their gold-flecked counterparts. "Are you sure?" he murmured.

She took an unsteady breath and nodded, lifting her arms to put them around his neck and pull him down to her. "I'm sure," she whispered. "Very, very sure."

With a husky groan, he lowered his lips to hers and parted her lips to let his tongue glide sensuously into her mouth. Her breath caught in her throat as his hand cupped her breast; then she felt his strong fingers begin to loosen the buttons of her shirt. She felt the coolness of his hand on her heated skin as he unclasped her bra and cupped her breast lovingly. His thumb moved erotically over her aroused nipple, and his rough calloused palm against her sensitive skin drove away any remaining doubts Jennie may have had.

His lips grazed across her cheek to her ear, where his teeth nibbled sensuously on her soft earlobe. She drew her breath in shakily and tightened her arms around Grady's neck, pulling him closer to her as his hand continued to massage her breast.

Delicious tremors shook her body as his lips lowered to her nipple and he began licking her softly, moistly.

"Ohh, Grady," she whispered. "It feels so good."

Slowly, as if reveling in each moment, Grady unzipped her jeans and began inching them down over her hips and along the smooth curves of her legs. They fell soundlessly to the floor, and she lay on the bed wearing only her bikini panties. Jennie watched as Grady began to undress. When his shirt sailed through the air to join her jeans on the floor, she chuckled throatily.

"What an incredible body you have," she whispered to him.

"And you, Jennie Winters, are the most wonderful woman in the world," he said as he shucked off the rest of his clothes and lay down beside her.

Grady's lips sought her breasts once again as his hands moved down over her hips to pull her closer. She reached out to touch his hardened manhood and heard his sharp intake of breath as she lightly stroked him with her fingers.

Grady pulled the bikini panties from her, then levered himself up and looked at her.

"My God," he whispered reverently. "You're perfect."

As one of his legs insinuated itself between hers, his hand was moving over her flat stomach and down into the soft curls at the V of her legs.

Jennie gasped when he found her moist center, then lay still to savor his touch as his hand moved sensuously, awakening every pore to the pleasure that was theirs. Wave after wave of desire flowed through her, rising in a crescendo until she cried out for him, but he delayed the moment, rubbing her as his tongue flicked erotically over her nipples.

"Oh!" she cried out. "Oh, please, Grady. I want you so badly."

She was on fire for him, rising in a need so powerful that it was like an earthquake inside her. Her hips arched, then rocked back and forth, but still he held off from the final joining. Slowly his lips trailed down, burning along the sensitive skin of her flat stomach and into the valley of her navel until he found her parted legs and nuzzled into her core.

"Ohhh," she groaned, fastening her hands in his hair and holding his head as his lips and tongue devoured her. Jennie felt weak with passion, and then, when she thought she could bear it no longer, he rose up and pulled her into his arms, uniting them with one fluid motion.

She received him joyfully, arching her hips to him and glorying in the feel of his hard body that joined hers in a love dance. Never, she thought, never have I felt this complete, this whole.

Jennie clung to him, her eyes squeezed shut, her head thrown back as her hair cascaded around her like a soft nimbus. She dug her hands into his broad, muscular back and urged him deeper. He answered her, falling into a perfect mutual rhythm that built to bring them to rapture's threshold again and again until he sent her hurtling over the edge of ecstasy into an abyss of total fulfillment.

As their breathing slowly returned to normal, they continued to hold each other, clinging as if they had been tossed in a storm. Grady finally eased himself from her and cradled her against his warm body, his hand reaching out to smooth her hair back from her face.

Jennie felt her lips curve into a soft smile. "Are you

going to make me get out of this bed and drive over to the schoolhouse *now*?"

He lay looking down at her, his eyes gleaming. "Not on your life. I've got you right where I want you, and I'm keeping you here as long as I can. Any objections?"

She looked up at him and felt the slow miracle of knowledge dawned on her. She felt totally right with this man. Grinning at him, she reached up and smoothed Grady's dark hair from his face.

"Not one, Mr. O'Hara. Only a suggestion."

"And that is?"

"Do it again," she whispered. "And this time don't stop so soon. . . ."

# Chapter Ten

❧

"Move in with you?" Jennie stared at Grady, a feeling of warmth spreading through her at his suggestion. "But . . ."

"But what, Jennie?" Grady asked. "It doesn't make sense for you to stay at that motel any longer. I want you here with me, sleeping with me at night, looking at me over breakfast in the morning. We can leave for the schoolhouse together. It's perfect—at least until the schoolhouse is ready for you to move into."

Jennie sat on the edge of Grady's bed, buttoning her shirt. Her jeans lay in a rumpled heap on the floor where Grady had tossed them. They had spent a delicious afternoon in bed, holding each other, laughing softly, talking, then making slow, languorous love. To Jennie it had been perfect. Looking at him now, she realized that she'd somehow stumbled onto the one man in the world who seemed to combine all the qualities she wanted in a man.

Dizzy with her discovery, she stood and picked up her jeans, then stepped into them, all the while thinking about what he'd just suggested. Looking up at him, she found herself smiling.

"You mean come here on Friday nights and stay until Sunday night?"

"Or better yet, until Monday morning. I want to have you as much as I can before you move into the schoolhouse."

"And when will that be?"

Grady rubbed his chin as he calculated the time. "Well, we have to finish the wallboard next week, then I'll start fixing up the sleeping loft. After that I'll have the plumber and cabinetmaker come in to work on the bathroom and kitchen." A slow grin crossed his face. "Let's say another month to six weeks, if I can work during the week occasionally." He drew her into his arms and lowered his lips to the ripe curve where her shoulder joined her neck. "That gives me six weekends of having you all to myself. It sounds like heaven."

She shivered as his hand cupped one breast. "It sounds wonderful to me, Grady. If it won't be any trouble . . ."

He grinned at her. "Oh, it'll be trouble—trouble getting out of bed Saturday and Sunday mornings, trouble getting to work on time at seven, trouble keeping my hands off you. There'll be plenty of trouble, all right."

Grinning back at him, she raised her arms and circled his neck, pulling his head down to kiss him. "I'm still your boss, Mr. O'Hara," she said softly. "And if I order you to stay in bed a little longer on Saturday or Sunday morning, I expect you to comply with my wishes. Is that understood?"

"Perfectly," he breathed, kissing her softly. "Perfectly."

\*     \*     \*

The following day, Jennie floated in to work. She sang out good morning to everyone she passed in the hall on the way from the elevator, then sailed into her office and immediately stooped to smell her plants. Inhaling their sweet scents, she felt like kicking her shoes off for joy and singing at the top of her lungs. She wanted to tell the entire world that she was in love with a man named Grady O'Hara and that for the next six weekends she'd be spending every possible moment with him. What would happen beyond that, she couldn't imagine, but for now there didn't have to be a future. The present seemed to be a miracle.

Her eyes fell on the invitation to John and Martha Powell's cocktail party. Taking her seat slowly, Jennie stared at it. Suddenly it didn't seem so impossible to ask Grady to go with her. One wonderful weekend had changed her entire perspective about him. He was no longer the carpenter she'd hired to renovate her week-end home, he was the man she loved. There was no question now that she would ask him to go with her. The only question was when she would ask him. Should she call now and hope to catch him home, or wait until next weekend?

Glancing at the clock, she realized that he would probably already be at the schoolhouse, starting his work on the drywall. He'd promised her that he would work a few days there during the week, so perhaps she should leave him alone and talk to him next weekend.

Putting the invitation down, she felt a sunburst of joy explode inside her. It seemed inconceivable, but in the space of two days, Jennie's entire life had changed. She had returned to her desk a new woman, and the magic was going to last, she could tell. There was too much joy with Grady for it to be a fluke. She'd finally found the love of a lifetime and she knew with calm certainty that everything from here on out would be perfect.

Humming softly, Jennie slipped her pocketbook into her desk drawer, then pulled out the report she'd been working on Friday. Bending her head, she was immersed in it at once, all thoughts of Grady and the future temporarily forgotten.

On Friday afternoon Jennie got held up by a last-minute conference, and she wasn't able to leave as early as she'd planned. Gnawing on the end of her pen, she glowered at the co-workers who held her here when she wanted to be with Grady at the schoolhouse. Finally, a half hour before the end of the workday, she was able to get away. She hurried to her car, where her suitcase was already stashed, then had to fight the lines of traffic edging out of Hartford toward Boston. It was a typical summer weekend and the line of cars seemed endless in front of her as she inched forward, then jammed on her brakes, then inched forward a few feet again. Progress was stop-and-go for a few miles; then the highway seemed to open up and she was on her way, singing jubilantly to herself as she drove, her face glowing with excitement at the prospect of spending an entire weekend with Grady.

When she arrived at the schoolhouse, she found him working on the drywall. When he saw her, he put down his hammer and took her into his arms, kissing her soundly while she laughingly explained why she was late.

"It's all right, honey," he said lovingly. "I realize

you've got an important job and can't be here every minute."

Thankfully she gazed up at him. "Say, O'Hara, do you realize you're a man in a million?"

"Don't go telling me that. I'll get a big head."

"But you are! What other man would be so understanding after I promised to be here to help you?"

He reached out and smoothed her hair back out of her eyes. "Hey, I understand that things happen to hold people up. Anyway, I've got you to myself all weekend, so I'm not going to complain if you're a few hours late on Friday afternoon."

That set the tone for the rest of the weekend. They worked together on the drywall, laughing and joking, then left the schoolhouse and barbecued steaks, sitting out under the stars and drinking red wine far into the night.

On Saturday Grady taught Jennie how to tape up the wallboard, then apply the compound over the tape, and when the compound dried, how to sand it so that the walls had a smooth, uniform finish. She spent the rest of the weekend doing that while Grady finished up the rough framing for the kitchen and bathroom.

It wasn't until she was driving home Sunday night that she remembered she hadn't asked Grady to go with her to the cocktail party. She shrugged it off. What did it matter? Naturally he'd want to go with her. She'd ask him next weekend, even though the party was only two weeks away.

But the following weekend, Jennie was so excited about being with Grady again that the party slipped her mind on Friday and Saturday. Their lovemaking held her in thrall all night and the work at the schoolhouse occupied her all day. It wasn't until Sunday when she was preparing to leave that she remembered the cocktail party. She and Grady had finished with work and were having iced tea on the back terrace of Grady's house. Totally relaxed, Jennie sat in a redwood chair opposite Grady, her head tilted back as she looked up at the sky through the overhanging branches of a tall maple.

"Oh! I almost forgot again! We have a party to go to next weekend."

Grady took a sip of his iced tea, then looked over at her. "A party? What do you mean?"

She grinned impishly. "Just what I said, Grady. We have a party to go to. A cocktail party. My boss and his wife have it every year. They're famous for it. There'll be fabulous food and good music and everyone dresses to the teeth. The place will be awash with good Scotch, Perrier, and white wine. You'll love it."

Grady's face grew still. "Not really, Jennie," he said slowly.

"Of course you will! It's fun, Grady, really. Very, *very* posh. I'll wear something that looks like it came out of *Vogue* and you can wear your best suit—"

"I don't own a suit." He sat in the chair opposite her, his face serious, staring at her with cool eyes.

Jennie's face fell; then she laughed. "Don't own a suit. Why, you must. Everyone owns a suit."

"*I* don't, Jennie," he said quietly, his eyes looking like blue glaciers.

She felt her smile drain away; then she forced it back on her face. "Grady, you're kidding me, aren't you?"

He shook his head. "No."

"But that's . . ." She laughed uncertainly. "Why, that's

absurd, Grady. Of course you must have at least one suit."

If it were possible, his eyes grew even colder. "Must I?" he asked coolly.

She felt her smile fade away, and this time she didn't try to force it back into place. "Oh, I see." Then she brightened. "Well, it doesn't matter. A nice sports jacket and slacks will do just as well. Or maybe we can go out and buy you a suit. If you don't have one, you can use it—there'll be other parties we'll have to go to for my job."

"I don't think you heard me, Jennie. I said I didn't own a suit. And I don't *want* to own one. Now or ever. When I left my job at the museum I chucked every damn suit I ever owned and I vowed that was the last I'd ever see of them. I meant it, Jennie." He shook his head slightly. "I'm not going to buy a suit, not to please you or anyone else on earth."

Jennie's face grew as cold as Grady's. "But I'm not just anyone, Grady," she said quietly. "I'm the woman who's been sharing your home. I thought I meant more to you than some casual acquaintance."

"You do," he said angrily. "You know you do. It's not a question of your not meaning anything to me, Jennie, it's a question of my wanting to choose how I dress and how I spend my time. After all those mandatory cocktail parties when I worked at the museum, I'm sick and tired of the damned things. I'd just as soon we forgot the party and stayed here next Saturday night."

She found herself sitting up straighter, her hands clenching the arms of the lawn chair. "And I'd just as soon that we went," she said quietly, an air of challenge in her words.

"Then we're at stalemate. I have no desire to go. Perhaps you'd better go alone."

She stared at him, uncertainty gnawing away inside her. "Grady," she said, laughing hesitantly, "this is ridiculous. I want to go to that party, and I want to go with you. Come with me. I'm sorry about the way I approached it, I had no idea you felt so strongly about it. If I'd known, I'd have . . ."

"Have what, Jennie?" he asked darkly. "Cuddled up in my lap and asked me in between kisses? Do you think it would've worked better if you softened me up first?"

"No!" She sat forward, her face bewildered by his vehemence. "Grady, no. I'd have been more tactful, that's all. I wouldn't have jumped to the conclusion that you'd want to go with me. I'd have . . ." She trailed off, fighting back tears. "Oh, never mind," she choked. "It doesn't matter what I'd have done."

"That's right, it doesn't, because I have no intention of going to the blasted party with you."

She found herself shaking, she was so angry. "You're being unreasonable, Grady. Completely unreasonable!"

"Am I? Is it unreasonable to want to have the right to decide for yourself what you do with your time?"

"Yes!" she almost shouted. "Yes, it is. I'm not asking you to go to Gibraltar with me, you know. I'm only asking that you go with me to a silly cocktail party. You'd think I was asking for the moon."

"To me, you are," he said shortly.

She closed her eyes and counted to ten, but it didn't help. Her anger was like a red cape to a bull, inflaming her, making her seethe with frustration.

"Grady, this isn't just a small argument over a silly party. This is really about you and me."

"Yes, I realize that, Jennie. It's about whether I have the right to decide how I want to spend my time. It's about whether you can *let* me decide for myself or whether you have to try to bend me to your wishes."

*"Bend* you?" She felt her cheeks growing scarlet, but there was no stopping her. "I'm not trying to bend you!"

"Then what would you call it?" He stood glaring at her, his hands curled into fists.

"I'm merely asking, Grady," she said, taking a deep breath and trying to calm down. "*Asking* that you go to a party that means a lot to me. Is that asking so very much?"

"Unfortunately, it is. I've told you how I feel about parties, Jennie. If you can't respect how I feel, then maybe we don't have much of a future together."

"A future?" she repeated. "What kind *could* we have? Parties are as much a part of my life as my job is. They're actually part of my job, as a matter of fact. I'm an insurance executive, Grady. I have all kinds of contacts who can further my career, and I meet them at all kinds of social activities. If you can't bring yourself to go with me, then . . ." She broke off, not wanting to face what she feared most.

"Then what, Jennie?" He stood before her, his face as unyielding as stone.

She shook her head and felt tears stinging her eyes, but she knew she mustn't cry. Somehow she had to hide her feelings, she couldn't let him see her disappointment and misgivings. She needed time to think about what had happened, time to sort out what everything meant and how it affected their relationship.

But Grady wasn't giving her time. He stood like a

rock, staring at her with glacial blue eyes, his hands shoved into his pockets, his arms stiff and unyielding.

"Then what, Jennie?" he pressed.

She took a deep breath, feeling her anger crumble, replaced by resignation. "Then perhaps we have no future, Grady," she said quietly. "Perhaps there's nothing between us but physical passion, and maybe we'd better not give in to that anymore."

"Is that your way of solving a problem, Jennie? By removing yourself from a man's bed until he complies with your wishes?"

"That's not what I said!" she cried, shaking again in her agitation.

"Isn't it? It sounds like it to me."

"Yes, but you've been misinterpreting everything I've said today, Grady," she said bitterly. "So why should this by any different?"

"Then tell me what you meant."

"I surely didn't mean that I'd try to use sex to force you to change your mind!" she retorted hotly.

"Then you're acting like a spoiled child. If you can't get your way, you're going to take your toys and go home, is that it?"

"No! That's not it at all! You're twisting everything I've said!"

"Then untwist it." He took his hands out of his pocket and folded his arms, waiting for her to speak.

She lifted her chin and glared at him, so angry that she wasn't sure she could trust herself to talk sensibly. She took a breath to calm down, then spoke.

"I merely said that there might be nothing between us but physical passion, Grady, and if that's the case, then I can't continue to live with you. You're refusing to do something that means a lot to me, so what possible future could we have together?"

"We won't find out if you move out, that's for sure. It seems to me the only way we can find out if we have a future is by trying to *make* one together. That means staying together and ironing out the problems, not running away from them."

"Who's running away?"

"You are!" he said roughly. "You're the one who wants to move out."

"Do you think I could stay with you after this?"

"Why not? We won't get anywhere if you stalk off and sulk."

"I am *not* sulking!" she cried, holding her clenched hands rigidly by her sides.

"Fine! Then go off by yourself and lick your wounds and see what the hell happens between us. If you want to find out about our future, you'll find out we don't have much of one this way, that's for sure."

"Then let me find it out," she said, lifting her chin to a defensive angle.

"All right, Jennie. If that's the way you want it, then that's how it will be."

She stared at him, feeling a sudden desire to run into his arms and cling to him; yet something held her back. Proudly she raised her chin even higher. "All right, Grady. That's how I want it."

# Chapter Eleven

Jennie was never more aware of Grady than she was during the next few weeks. Every time she looked at him she felt a curling sensation in the pit of her stomach. Her hands itched to reach out and touch him, to slide over the wiry hairs on his muscled chest. Her fingers wanted to smooth back his thick hair, to touch his chiseled lips and sink into the bronzed skin of his back. She wanted nothing more than to lie against him, inhaling his fresh scent and feasting her eyes on his beloved face.

But she could do none of those, except look at him from a distance. Work on the schoolhouse progressed rapidly now, for Grady worked like a demon, hardly acknowledging Jennie as he put up the wallboard for the kitchen and bathroom. Jennie stood alongside, handing him the nails he needed, remembering how different it was when they had done this in the living room; they had laughed and joked and stolen an occasional kiss.

Now she raised her chin combatively and sniffed. "You're not very talkative today, Mr. O'Hara," she said coolly. "Cat got your tongue?"

He glanced at her with equal coolness. "Something like that," he said, his eyes stony.

"Look, just because we're not sleeping together anymore isn't any reason for us not to talk, you know."

"Isn't it?" He hammered in a nail, not looking at her, then reached for another.

"No," she said, glaring at him. "It isn't."

"What do you suggest we do? Act as if nothing has happened?"

"Why not? It'd be a far sight better than this. It's so cold around here, this may as well be an igloo."

"It seems to me you're the one who wanted to move out, Ms. Winters. You'll just have to put up with it."

She put her hands on her hips and stomped her foot. "Grady! Look at me, dammit!"

He swung his head around and gazed at her with cool eyes. "What's the matter, Jennie? Can't take it?"

"Not when you act so childishly," she snapped.

He sighed and rubbed his chin. "All right, we'll make peace."

She felt herself begin to relax. "Okay. That sounds better."

His eyes drifted over her figure, pausing at her breasts, then rising to her eyes once again. "But don't hold me responsible if I get carried away."

Jennie raised her chin a quarter of an inch. "Don't be foolish, Grady. You're a grown man. You can control your . . . your animal impulses."

One corner of his mouth quirked up. "Animal impulses? Is that what they are?"

She tossed her head. "Yes. What else could you call mere physical attraction?"

"Lust," he drawled. "Carnal desire."

"Well, whatever you call it, control it," she said haughtily.

"Ah, Jennie Winters, if only it were that easy," he said, smiling wistfully. "You seem to think I'm made of stone."

"You acted like you were last weekend," she snapped.

"You malign me," he said mockingly. "I was merely acting out of self-defense. It was your idea to move out, remember? I wanted to try to reach some sort of understanding between us."

Jennie snorted. "What kind of understanding could we have reached, Grady? I don't call it much of an understanding when I do all the giving in and you do all the getting."

"Did I ask you to give in to me?"

"No, but that's what you implied!" Her voice rose. "You were saying in so many words: stay with me but don't expect me to compromise."

Grady put down his hammer and turned to face her squarely. He reached out and put his hands on her shoulders as if he were going to shake her. "Look, Jennie. It's like this. I didn't like the way you casually *assumed* that I'd go with you, the way you casually *assumed* I had a suit, or would want to buy one to please you."

"So that's what it's about! It's not about the party at all, is it, Grady? You just didn't like me assuming that you'd go with me." She put her hands on her hips and shook off his hands. "Well, I don't think it was such a big assumption to make, Grady. It seemed relatively normal to me that you'd *want* to go out with me. Do you think a woman likes to stay home all the time? I'd kind of like to go out, you know. Didn't you ever hear of taking a woman to the movies or out to dinner?"

"You want dinner, you'll get dinner. How about tonight? At the Publick House in Sturbridge."

"I can't tonight, Grady. Tonight's the cocktail party."

"Ah, yes, the infamous cocktail party. The very thing that started this mess."

"That's right. I'm leaving here at five to go and get ready. It'll take me about an hour to get to Simsbury from here." She cocked her head and smiled. "Sure you don't want to go? Last chance."

To her surprise, he grinned at her. Then he shook his head. "You go on alone, Jennie. I really meant it when I said I don't like parties much."

"All right, but about dinner . . ."

"Next Saturday?"

She smiled at him. "Next Saturday it is."

She was nervous all week, and especially so on Saturday when they worked together. What would they talk about while they ate? They still weren't completely comfortable together, even at the schoolhouse. Jennie stared at Grady and wondered what was going through his mind. Whatever it was, it made him happy, for as he worked upstairs in the attic, preparing the loft area, he was whistling again.

By the time five o'clock came, Jennie had finished stripping the old paint from all the downstairs windows and Grady was still at work upstairs.

"Grady?" she called up to him.

"Yes?" He came to the stairs and stood looking down at her.

"I'm leaving now. What time are our reservations tonight?"

"Seven. I'll pick you up at about six-forty-five."

She nodded, then stood on the first step and stared up at him. He had taken off his shirt and she could see the sweat glistening on his muscled chest. Suddenly she felt a pang in the middle of her stomach and had to put a hand out and hold on to the wall. She could almost feel his hard body, could almost feel the wiry hairs under her hand and the warmth of him.

"I . . . I'll see you then," she said, and backed away, still staring up at him, as if caught in a trance.

"Till then," he said softly.

She nodded, then swallowed hard and turned to rush away, wanting to hurl herself at him but knowing she couldn't. As she drove off in her car, she realized she was trembling, shaking from the sight of his nearly naked body.

Jennie sat in the tub, soaking in the mounds of suds, her eyes closed in complete relaxation. Her hair was tied on top of her head, but small tendrils had escaped in the steamy room, softly framing her face. On the bed, her best dress was laid out, a red silk creation that buttoned down the front and flared around her knees. The soft chiffon sleeves billowed around her slim arms, and she would wear her high-heeled black sandals with it.

For now, she was content to luxuriate in the tub and let the time pass, unconcerned with clock-watching. Sighing, she opened her eyes and did what she didn't want to do, looked at the clock. Her eyes widened when she saw that it was already six-fifteen. Grady would be here in half an hour and she still had to dress and do her hair.

Putting on her laciest underwear, Jennie could feel her heartbeat begin to palpitate from nerves. As she pulled on her dress, she glanced in the mirror and saw that her cheeks were red from excitement and her eyes glowed.

"No makeup for you, my girl," she said out loud, and found herself grinning at herself.

Her hands shook as she combed her hair, letting it cascade halfway down her back in a tumble of wild curls. Standing back, she ran a critical eye over her appearance and realized she'd forgotten her pearls. There was a light knock on the door just as she picked them up. Her eyes flew to the clock. If it was Grady, he was five minutes early.

She hurried to the door and pulled it open, then stood and stared at him.

"Hello, Grady. You're early."

He wore a white shirt and black trousers and she realized this was the first time she'd ever seen him wearing something other than jeans. Her eyes slid over him and she found her pulse jumping erratically at the sight. His muscled body wore the clothes with an easy grace, his wide shoulders and broad chest straining the light material of the shirt, his strong thighs bulging under the black trousers.

When her gaze came back to his face, she realized with a start that he was inspecting her as well, his deep blue eyes running down her figure slowly, with the ease and thoroughness of a connoisseur. When his eyes met hers, she felt a jolt like electricity coursing through her body.

"Do I pass inspection?" she asked, her voice oddly throaty.

His eyes glittered warmly. "More than pass," he said, then reached out and took the pearls from her nerveless fingers. "Let me," he said, and reaching out, put his hands on her shoulders and gently turned her around. She shivered as she felt his hand take the heavy weight of her hair and lift it as he circled her neck with the pearls. "Bend your head," he murmured and, like a doll, she obeyed.

The touch of his fingers was like a whisper on the nape of her neck. Trembling, Jennie stood rooted to the floor, hot flashes of desire pulsing through her. Somehow it felt strangely erotic to have him standing behind her, clasping her pearls. It was as if he were undressing her instead.

When he finished with the pearls, Grady slid his hands down to her shoulders, then lowered his lips and let them graze the sensitive skin on her neck.

Her breath shook in her body as she inhaled. Jennie knew she should move away from him, but she couldn't. She stood and let him kiss her neck, shivering when his hands slid slowly down her arms and around her waist to pull her against his warm, strong body.

Her breathing quickened and she knew that her heartbeat was thudding in her breast. Jennie wondered if he could hear it. Grady's hands were flat against her midriff, splayed over her body. He moved his thumbs softly so that they were just brushing the undersides of her breasts, while his lips grazed sensuously on her neck, then traveled slowly to her earlobe.

Jennie was helpless to stop her errant reactions. Everything seemed out of control, lost in a storm of desire.

She smelled the heady scent of Grady's after-shave as he turned her to face him. Before she knew it, Jennie was in his arms, her head bent back as his lips savored hers.

Shakily she brought her arms up and pushed against his chest, then turned her head away from his drugging kiss.

"Grady," she whispered. "It's late . . ."

"Ahhh, Jennie," he murmured, his lips nibbling again at her ear. "It's never too late, darlin'."

Hazily she realized that he was misinterpreting her words. "No," she protested weakly. "I mean we'll be late." She took a deep breath and let it out on a sigh. "For dinner."

"Dinner enough here," he murmured, his tongue flicking into her ear and sending sparks of hot firelike desire shooting through her stomach. "All I want to eat is right here," he whispered.

Melting warmth coursed through her veins. She spread her palms over his chest, then pushed the tips of her fingers between the buttons of his shirt and found the warm, hair-roughened skin she knew so well. His hands ran up her back as he pulled her closer to the hard strength of his body.

"Jennie," he whispered. "I want you."

The truth of his words was evident in the hard outline of his male desire pressing into her stomach. But she couldn't let it happen. She pushed hard against his chest and then stood with her arms out, holding him off.

"No, Grady," she said, her voice quivering slightly. "We have reservations in a few minutes."

For a moment she didn't think he would listen to her,

but then he nodded. "All right. If it's dinner you want, it's dinner you'll get."

She stared at him, hearing the resigned bitterness in his voice, and a sudden feeling of dismay swept through her. Why had she spoken? Why couldn't she have let it happen? They had been about to make love. That would have solved all their problems. Now she was back where she had started, and Grady was looking like a storm cloud.

He took her arm and swept her out of the motel room, banging the door shut behind them. Jennie had to hurry to keep up with his pace. He walked hurriedly toward his truck, which sat looking as old and disreputable as it always did.

Jennie stopped short. "Grady, don't you even own a *car?*" she asked heatedly.

He turned to her and glared. "No, Ms. Winters. I have no need for a car. Why? Isn't this good enough for you? Do you want me to go out and buy a car now? Just to please your whims?"

"It's hardly a whim," she snapped, taking hold of her skirt and staring down at the precious red silk. "My dress is going to get filthy."

Grady sighed exaggeratedly, then stood glaring at her. "So what would you like me to do about it? Spread a cape over the seat for milady?"

She felt her cheeks beginning to get red as her hands knotted into fists. "No," she said stiffly. "I wouldn't dream of expecting you to act like a gentleman."

She saw a muscle begin to work in his jaw and knew that he was barely holding his temper in check. "Damnit, Jennie, how was I to know you'd wear that frilly thing?"

"What did you expect?" she asked coolly. "Blue jeans?"

He groaned and stood rubbing his chin; then he sighed and ran his hand back through his hair. "Well, there's nothing else to do," he said resignedly. "We'll have to take your car."

"Oh." She felt her mouth begin to relax into a smile. "Oh, that's right, we can take my car."

"Are you happy now?" he asked sarcastically.

Her smile immediately dissipated. "Grady, will you get that chip off your shoulder?"

He took her arm and guided her toward her car. "It's not a chip, Jennie. It's a tree stump."

She felt her lips begin to shake with silent laughter. "Well, at least you admit it."

"Dammit, what do you expect? A couple weeks ago you acted as if I were from some primitive island because I don't own a suit. Then you stomp off mad and refuse to stay at my place any longer. Tonight, when I kiss you, you push me away and remind me about dinner. Then you see my truck and berate me for not owning a car! Can't I do anything right with you?"

"The kiss was all right," she said softly.

He stood and looked down into her eyes. "Then why did you push me away?"

"Maybe because I didn't trust myself." Her voice was almost a whisper.

He reached out and smoothed her hair back from her face. "Then trust me, Jennie. Trust *me*."

She felt a shiver go through her. "I'll try, Grady."

Slowly his head lowered to hers, as his lips brushed gently against her lips. "That's all I ask, Jennie. . . ."

\*     \*     \*

As they sat in the candlelit restaurant with hand-hewn beams and timber stalls turned into booths, Jennie gazed across at Grady, trying to fathom the man.

"You must have really been bitter when Laura left you, Grady. Is that why you threw out all your suits?"

He sighed and drank some of his beer. "I suppose it's one reason, Jennie. She was such a social climber, always after me to make something of myself. When I left the museum job, I decided I was leaving that kind of life forever. I was in a rage that day and I threw out all the three-piece suits I owned, swearing I'd never go back."

"And when I asked you to go to the party with me," Jennie said gently, "did you think I was asking you to go back to it?"

He stared down at his beer glass, then glanced up at her. "I guess I did, Jennie. I reacted as if I was stung, I know that."

"Did I . . . ?" Jennie hesitated, then forced herself to go on. "Did I remind you of Laura?"

He looked directly into her eyes. "Yes, I think you did. You were talking about this posh party and you sounded so excited. All I could hear was Laura talking about the parties we used to go to. It threw me for a loop, Jennie."

She nodded. "Yes, I can see how it could. But, Grady—"

"No, you're not anything like her. She's blond, one of those cool, classic types with ice water in her veins. She never yells or gets mad, she just grows cold and distant. No, Jennie, you could never be like Laura in a million years."

She smiled at him. "How did you know I was going to ask that?"

"I could tell by the look on your face. You looked so unhappy, as if you were being compared with her." He shrugged.

Jennie nodded thoughtfully. "You know, your description of Laura reminds me of another woman I've heard about. Eleanor Avery."

Grady smiled. "Ah, Eleanor." He nodded. "Yes, she's very much like Laura. They're both the classic platinum blond. Very beautiful. Very bewitching. Thank God I'd had my fill of Laura when I met Eleanor or there would have been hell to pay."

"In what way?" She stared across at him, interested for some reason that she couldn't explain.

"Eleanor is a very beautiful woman, Jennie. Even more beautiful than Laura, if that's possible. And she's really interested in historic restoration. Naturally, that's quite a combination to me. When I first met Eleanor it was pretty obvious that she was coming on to me, and I was tempted, believe me. She'd smile into my eyes and reach out and touch my arm and I'd almost give in, but Laura always stepped between us like a shadow."

"Laura? Why Laura?"

"Because I'd lived with a woman like Eleanor and knew the havoc she could create. Every time I was tempted by Eleanor, I remembered Laura. That's what kept me sane."

"Dana's still half in love with her, you know."

He nodded grimly. "Dana's a fool. He's caught in her spell and can't get out. Four years ago, when Eleanor left him, I told him to forget her, but he's still holding a torch." He cocked his head to one side and stared questioningly at Jennie. "How do you know about Dana and Eleanor?"

"I went by his house about a month ago and we had dinner. Afterward he told me all about her—and about you and her."

"*Me* and her? There never was a me and Eleanor, Jennie."

"I know. That seemed to bother him. He couldn't believe there was a man on earth who could resist Eleanor when he couldn't."

"I see." Grady nodded thoughtfully, then smiled at her. "But that's not important. It *is* important that you were with Dana, though."

"Oh." She waved a dismissing hand. "No, really, it isn't important. I just stopped by and we got to talking . . ."

"And you're not interested in him? He's a pretty rich man. He owns all kinds of suits. And an expensive car."

She smiled and shook her head. "Yes, he does, but he doesn't tempt me in the least."

"Do I? That's the important question."

She smiled and ran her finger around the rim of her glass. "Yes, Grady. That's the problem—you tempt me too much. And I don't know how to handle it right now."

"Handle it by going home with me tonight and staying with me on the weekends."

She shook her head. "No. That's not the way. Don't you see, Grady? The only way we seem to know how to solve our problems is with sex, and that won't work all the time. We can't just kiss and make up and expect that everything will be rosy. There has to be another way to try to solve things."

"But, Jennie, what other way is there if we're not together in the first place?"

She stared into her glass, then picked it up and sipped her white wine. "You know," she said after a few moments, "the one thing we seem to have is an incredible physical attraction. Every time I see you I begin to shake. But, Grady . . ." She tried to search for the words she needed to explain her fears. "That's not going to be enough. We'll need more than just good sex if we're to have any kind of life together."

"You miss my point, Jennie. How will we know unless we try to make a life together? Come back and live with me, at least until the schoolhouse is finished. That way we can work at it. This way there's no chance for us to get to know each other better."

She sat and considered his words, but something held her back. Deep inside she had grave fears about a future with Grady. How could they ever make a life together? They were too different, their life-styles were completely at odds. And even deeper, they were both stubborn; neither knew how to give in to the other. Until they found a way around those problems, they had little hope of ever being truly happy.

"Grady," she said finally, "I can't. I need time, time to think things out. I won't be able to do that if I live with you on the weekends. Give me some time, Grady. Don't be angry with me, please, try to understand. Try to see my viewpoint. I'm afraid . . ."

"Afraid of what?"

"I . . . I don't really know. I just know that I can't live with you right now. I need some time and distance. Can you give me that?"

He ran a hand through his hair, then nodded. "Yes,

Jennie," he said quietly. "I can give you as much time as you need."

When he brought her back to her motel an hour and a half later, he left her at the door without kissing her. Jennie went inside and closed the door, then leaned back on it and closed her eyes. She wasn't surprised a few minutes later when she realized she was crying.

# Chapter Twelve

Through the long, hot month of August, the work continued on the schoolhouse. When the walls were finished,
Grady stripped the living-area floors in preparation for
refinishing. Then he worked on the kitchen and bathroom,
readying them for the plumber, electrician, and cabinetmaker. By the time the plumbing was in and the wiring
done, he had completed the greenhouse addition off the
kitchen. During the week, a mason worked on the chimney and hearth for the wood stove and a stairmaker
made the new stairs up to the sleeping area on the
second floor.

Every weekend when Jennie showed up, something
new had been done. She was torn between her excitement with the house and disappointment with Grady.
He was taking her at her word and she found she didn't
like it. When they worked together, he was all business,
as stiff and proper with her as if they'd never shared a
meal, much less a bed.

But as his indifference toward her continued, Jennie
became increasingly aware of him. Trying to strip
woodwork, she would find herself looking up and follow-

ing him with her eyes, noting how his shirt stretched across his broad shoulders or how the buttons were undone halfway from the top. At those times, her stomach would turn a somersault and she'd have to look away, careful to school her features to remain calm, not revealing her inner turmoil.

Not only was she aware of Grady on the weekends, working alongside him; she was also aware of him during the week. She would find herself sitting at her desk remembering something he had said or done and ten minutes later she would still be dreaming about him, unable to keep her mind on her work.

And all the while she was increasingly aware of September's rapid approach. In September, Grady assured her, the schoolhouse would be finished. And the unspoken understanding was that in September she would have had the time she needed and would make some kind of decision about them.

But as September approached, she had no time to think about Grady. She was snowed under at work by a project which she'd been given complete authority over. John Powell told her that if it went well, it could mean another promotion for her, and so she worked doggedly, forcing herself to concentrate even when she would have liked to think about Grady.

Then suddenly Grady was telling her that she could move into the schoolhouse.

"The plumbing's in, the wiring's done. There's no reason why you can't move in now. What little finish work that needs to be done can be done after you move in."

Jennie stared at him. "Oh, but I can't! I have a party to go to next weekend, and I have to be there. It's important, all my clients will be there."

Grady shrugged. "Move in first, then go to your party. Where is it, anyway? In Simsbury again?"

"No, this one's in Hartford, at a restaurant. It's the culmination of the project I'm working on. Since I'm in charge of the project, I have to go to the party."

"Well, the schoolhouse is ready for you. It's up to you when you want to move in."

In the end, she decided to do it that weekend. She took Friday off and rented a trailer to attach to her car. A neighbor helped her load the few pieces of furniture that she would need; then she drove off toward Stockton, excitement burgeoning inside her.

Grady was at the schoolhouse to help her unload the furniture, and he too seemed to share her mood. His distance was gone, and he was grinning with her, laughing infectiously, happy that she was moving in. When Jennie tried to figure out his new mood, she was unable to. She was only happy that he was acting this way. It made moving in that much more fun.

It took an hour and a half to get her bed, a dresser, a couch, chairs, and a kitchen table inside. It was a typical August day, and by the time they were finished, they were both tired and sweaty.

"There's lemonade in my thermos," Grady said. "Let's go sit outside and cool off. We deserve a break."

"That sounds terrific." Jennie followed him out back to a tall maple tree and they sat under it.

"To your new home," he said, holding up a paper cup of lemonade.

"To my home," she responded, and they touched cups, then drank greedily, laughing as the lemonade splashed onto their chins.

She lay back on the grass and looked up through the

trees and sighed contentedly. "I still have to make up the bed and find the box with all my towels."

Grady grunted, sounding equally contented. "You can do that tonight. Let's just stay here all afternoon and enjoy the peace, Jennie. God, it's a wonderful place you've got here. Peace and quiet and solitude all around us. Not another soul for miles." He smiled lazily and looked across at her. "I'm glad you've moved in, Jennie. It's good to know the schoolhouse is almost ready."

"How much longer before everything is done?"

"Well, we'll have to move the couch and living-room chairs out to refinish the floors and paint the walls, then I'll have to do some finishing in the kitchen and upstairs in the sleeping area. We still have to paint the outside. That'll mean scraping it down and washing it with a mildew solution before we paint. So I'd say everything should be done by the last weekend in September. Maybe before if we can work over Labor Day weekend."

"That's only next weekend. Where's the summer gone?"

Grady grinned at her. "Into carpentry and stripping woodwork and plumbing, that's where it's gone."

She grinned back at him, falling into a comfortable silence. Everything seemed suddenly right. She was at ease with Grady as they'd been during the wonderful days when she'd lived with him. Lying on the grass, she closed her eyes and knew that her lips were curved into a soft, serene smile. As she lay there, she began to remember the days she had shared with Grady—the laughter and the fun they had had, the kisses, the passion and excitement. She began to feel faint stirrings at the memories.

"Jennie . . ." Grady looked over at her from his place under the tree.

"Mmm?"

"I'm remembering that first day you came to my place for brunch. Remember?"

She sighed shakily and nodded. "Yes, Grady, I was remembering, too."

"It was good, wasn't it?" he asked, sounding drowsy.

"Yes, Grady, very good."

He slid down along the ground until he was next to her, and her breathing suddenly became constricted. A powerful urge to turn into his arms and smother him with kisses almost overcame her, but she resisted with effort, trembling as he reached out and touched a strand of her hair.

"I want those days back again, Jennie," he whispered. His warm eyes gazed into hers.

"I do too, Grady," she whispered back as the familiar delicious tremors begin to shake her. "I do too."

She closed her eyes, increasingly aware of the throbbing in her breasts and the pulsing that had started between her legs. Taking a shaky breath, she opened her eyes and saw that Grady was still watching her. His deep blue eyes seemed to read everything in her mind. She lay quietly, returning his gaze, and Jennie felt the question lying heavy in the air between them: would it happen again? Would that incredible surge of physical attraction overpower them once more, giving rout to all her fine resolutions? She had vowed it wouldn't happen, yet here they were, surrounded by miles of solitude, and his blue eyes were boring into hers, turning her limbs to quivering need. She knew that she had vowed it wouldn't happen again, that she should get up and stop it from happening, but something held her back, something elemental within her, an instinct as old as time. She wanted Grady. It was as simple and as complex as that. And if that was wrong, then it seemed to her that everything in life was wrong; to join with this man, to give herself willingly and take what he gave in return, was the very essence of life, was what gave Jennie's life meaning. Looking into Grady's eyes was like looking into a fire; she felt filled with a warm and golden light. A smile grew on her face and she felt a rush of tenderness spreading through her, lifting her like the voices of a heavenly choir. It broke over her in a flood of happiness, drawing her forward to lean over him and gaze down into his eyes.

Reaching out, she slid her hand inside his shirt and caressed the hair-roughened surface of his skin. Jennie smiled as an incredible happiness welled up inside her; it was as if she, alone in the universe, had discovered the source of joy. Leaning down, she kissed him gently, moving her lips slowly over his, savoring the softness and taste of him.

His arms came up around her, pulling her down onto his chest. His mouth covered hers in hot passion, opening over hers, his tongue inserting itself into her mouth, tangling with hers in a rapturous dance.

Jennie felt shaken to her core by the symbolic mating, then gave herself up to the soft, hot kisses he rained on her. She felt her muscles go lax, felt her entire body melt into his as he rolled over on top of her with a murmur of pure satisfaction.

Grady's lips teased hers with soft kisses. Her breath was uneven and her body began to move instinctively, her hips arching against the hard outline of his male need. She moved her hands down his back and pulled his shirt from his jeans, then slid her hands under it to caress the silken smoothness of the gently shifting muscles in his back.

His mouth never left hers as he levered himself up to unbutton the rest of his shirt and pull it off. Then his fingers went to work on her buttons, slowly teasing one after the other and gently grazing her sensitive skin. When he had undone them all, Grady took off her shirt and unclasped her bra. The weight of her breasts was freed from the lacy confines; then she felt the warm strength of his palms cupping her left breast. She groaned and pulled him closer, her hands sliding up into the thick blackness of his hair.

His lips explored Jennie's neck, traveling down the thin ivory column to the soft hollow at the base of her throat. She felt her nipple rising firm and pink into the warm center of his callused palm as he began to slowly and sensuously massage it. When the nipple was hard and fully erect, he moved his thumb back and forth, scraping its hardness against the taut nipple until she thought she would scream in ecstasy.

Her breath shook in her body and her lips trembled against the warmth of Grady's chest. Jennie was blazingly aware of the hard bulge in his jeans and of the hot pulsing that radiated from between her legs.

With his hand still on her left breast, he moved his mouth to the hard center of her other one. Liquid heat exploded inside her, rushing through her body in waves and rippling down her abdomen to her soft, yearning center. She groaned, a sound halfway between ecstasy and pain, and threw back her head, holding his head to her breast as his mouth and tongue feasted on the pink bud.

"Ohhhh," she moaned, a sound soft and low, filled with that painful rapture. She never wanted it to end. She wanted this heaven to go on forever, to feel his hard body against hers, his strong hand caressing her, his warm mouth devouring her nipples, licking and pulling softly with his lips.

Jennie opened her eyes and looked straight up through the overhanging branches to the sky, the same sky that had witnessed their lovemaking once before.

*And it's happening again,* she thought. It was happening again and she was powerless to stop it. But she wouldn't stop it if she could. It was too beautiful—a rich, soaring symphony of love and passion and desire.

Grady knelt over her and gently peeled her jeans down her legs, then leaned forward and kissed her midriff. His lips adored her even as his fingers inserted themselves into the waistband of her bikini panties and pulled them off. When he stood up and removed his own clothing, she lay on the ground and stared up at him. The sight of his proud beautiful body made her ache with need, and she trembled with anticipation.

But he was in no hurry. He lowered himself beside her and kissed her gently. "Beautiful," Grady whispered. "You are so beautiful."

His right hand traced the pink areola of her breast, his fingertips a whisper on her sensitive skin. Jennie gasped at the pleasure he gave her. His fingers trailed slowly down her stomach; then he splayed them over her abdomen. She turned to face him, almost losing her breath as his hand slid between her thighs.

"Oh, yes," she whispered.

She opened to his fingers, soft and warm and moist, and was filled with the wild sweet music of rapture.

"Oh!" she gasped. "Oh, yess . . ."

Grady knelt between her parted thighs, then slid his hands beneath her as he filled her with a gentle fluid motion. His teeth bit into her earlobe with the softness of a caress, and Jennie felt herself slipping beyond the realm of conscious thought.

"Jennie," he whispered, saying her name over and over again as if it were a magic incantation. "Jennie. Oh, God, Jennie, Jennie . . ."

He pulled her closer to his quivering body, plunging even deeper as his hands lifted her to his urgent need. Lost and abandoned in their own private world, they melded together, riding their ever-increasing spirals of need. They held each other tightly, two joined as one as they neared the summit of their desire. And when it seemed that they might die from the beauty of it, when it seemed that they would burst, their release came, shattering fine golden splinters around them and breaking over them in pulsing waves of contentment and beauty.

A moment passed; then Jennie opened her eyes and looked into Grady's. "Oh, I love you, Grady O'Hara," she murmured, running her hands up his back and into his thick black hair. "God, how I love you."

He smiled into her eyes, then leaned down to kiss her gently. "And I love you, Jennie."

The smile grew on her face, lighting her amber eyes. "You're a wonderful man, do you know that?"

He shook his head, laughing lazily as he continued to kiss her. "Hush, Jennie Winters, or my head will grow too big."

She laughed out loud, squeezing her arms around him. "Oh, Grady, what's been *wrong* with me? Whatever was I doing, staying away from you so long?"

"Well, to tell you the truth, that's been worrying me, too. I've been afraid you didn't care."

"Didn't care?" she echoed, laughing with him. "I care so much I don't know how to tell you." She lay in his arms and looked up at him. "But let me try. You know how big the Grand Canyon is?" He nodded, leaning to kiss her. "Well, that's how much I love you. You know how big the Pacific Ocean is?" He laughed and nodded again. "Well, that's how much I love you." She screwed up her face and considered for a moment. "You know how big the universe is?" He shook his head at her, still laughing. "Well, that's how much I love you."

Grady gathered her into his arms and showered kisses on her. "And that's how much I love you, Jennie Winters."

"Really?" she asked, holding him away from her to look into his clear blue eyes. "You really do?"

"I really do. In fact, I've been giving considerable thought to asking you to marry me."

She grew serious as she lay looking up at him. "Marry?"

He smiled. "Marry me. Will you?"

She took a deep breath, then nodded. "Yes, I will."

He smoothed his hand back along her forehead gently. "Good. When?"

"Whenever you say. Tomorrow? The day after?"

"You're not in too much of a hurry, are you?" he asked, laughing softly.

She shook her head. "No. I just want to make sure you don't change your mind, that's all."

"I'll never do that. I'm just worried you might change your mind."

"No way. I know a good thing when I see it."

He looked at her, his eyes serious. "What made you change your mind? What happened?"

"It just happened, Grady, just now, when we made love," she answered quietly. "Suddenly everything seemed right with you. I wasn't afraid anymore."

"But what were you afraid of in the first place?" He sat up and began to pull on his clothes.

She took her time in replying, pulling on her own clothes as she considered his question. "Commitment, I think, Grady. And you."

"Me?" He stared at her. "Why were you afraid of me?"

"Oh, Grady," she said, buttoning her shirt. "You're so different from all of the men I've known. You swept me off my feet that first day by the pond, and I haven't known what was happening to me ever since. You frightened me, Grady. You and the emotions you created in me. Here I was, this sensible career woman, used to living her life by a five-year plan, always in control, and you came into my life like a thunderbolt. You shook me out of my complacency and overturned everything I believed I wanted in a man."

"Such as?"

"Oh . . ." She grinned at him. "Men who wear three-piece suits and parties."

"Ah . . ." He cocked his head and looked at her closely. "Now we come to the crux of the matter—three-iece suits and parties."

"What about them?"

"Are you sure you know what you want, Jennie? Are

you sure you can live with a man who doesn't own a suit? Who won't go with you to parties?"

"It's not a question of living with a man like that, it's a question of living without him. I suddenly realized that I can't live without you, Grady. I want you and I love you just the way you are, suits or no suits, parties or no parties."

"But it would mean going by yourself after we're married."

"*After* we're married? What are you talking about? I've got a party tomorrow night that I have to go to alone." She grinned at him. "But I'll live. If you will." It was her turn to question him. "Can you live with a woman who has to go out alone at night? Not every night, and not every weekend, but it'll happen, Grady. Can you live with that?"

His slow grin warmed her very soul. "It's not a question of living with it, Jennie Winters. It's more a case of not being able to live without you."

She smiled back at him, then tucked her hand in his arm and they began to walk together. "Are you sure?"

"Yes. Positive."

She sighed contentedly, then turned her head to look at him. "You really want to marry me?"

"Yes, I really do." He grinned down at her. "Why? Don't you believe me?"

"I'm just wondering where we're going to live when this marriage takes place. Am I going to stay in the schoolhouse on weekends and see you then, or what?"

He stopped and turned to put his hands on her shoulders. "Wait a minute, Jennie. We'll live together. You'll live with me and sleep with me, every night of the year, not just on weekends."

"Your place or mine?" she asked, laughing up at him.

"Ours." He leaned down and kissed her, then pulled her into his arms and squeezed her hard.

"Ours? What's that mean?"

"Well, I've been doing a lot of thinking, Jennie. While you were staying at that damnable motel in Sturbridge and I was sleeping alone, I thought a lot about what I wanted—"

"Did you, now?"

"I did. And you know what I've been thinking?"

"Haven't a clue."

"I've been thinking that my place is awful big for one person. It's even big for two people."

"What about two people, a dog, and a cat?"

"A cat?"

She nodded. "I haven't told you about my cat back in West Hartford. Her name's Ragamuffin and my neighbors have been taking care of her for me on weekends."

"Kaiser will be put out."

"So will Ragamuffin."

He grinned at her. "Anyway, I've been thinking that what a married couple needs is a small place with a wood stove, and a greenhouse addition, and one large bedroom—maybe an old schoolhouse would be nice."

"Funny you should mention a schoolhouse—I've got a nice one here. Think you'd like to live in it?"

"If you were living in it, yes."

"Otherwise?"

"Otherwise what's the sense? I want *you*, Jennie Winters, not your schoolhouse."

"Well, you're in luck, because we come as a pair."

"With a cat," he reminded her.

"Yes, with a cat. But then, you come with a dog, so we're even."

He leaned down to kiss her; then he released her and they started walking toward the schoolhouse. "But now comes the hard part, Jennie."

"The hard part? What do you mean?"

"It's going to be a long commute for you to go to work every day from here. I don't want to hear about you staying with me only on weekends. I want this to be our home, all year round."

She grinned at him. "Well, of course, silly. Did you really think I'd want to keep my apartment?"

"Well, you have to admit it is a long way into Hartford from here."

"Yes, it is, but there are commuter buses I can take, or car pools that I can get into. I met a guy a few weeks ago who commutes from Putnam. It can be done."

He pulled her into his arms and silenced her with a long kiss, then raised his head and looked down into her eyes. "Hey, Jennie Winters . . ."

"Mmm?"

"Do you know how much I love you?"

She shook her head.

"You know how big the Grand Canyon is?" She grinned up at him and nodded. "That's how much I love you. You know how big the Pacific Ocean is?" She nodded again, laughing softly. "That's how much I love you."

"You're not very original, Grady O'Hara."

"Yeah, but what I lack in originality, I make up for in ardor."

"Mmmm," she whispered, stretching up to kiss him. "I'll take ardor any day."

It was a lingering kiss; then Grady pulled away. "You know, Jennie, there's still one thing that worries me."

Concerned, she stared up at him. "What's that?"

"Well, you know how you said you've adjusted to my not owning a suit and not wanting to go to parties with you?"

"Yes."

"Well, there's only one thing wrong."

Her eyes widened in alarm as she waited to hear something she was afraid to hear. "What is it, Grady?" she asked softly. "Is it . . . ?"

"Well, it's like this, Jennie. I got to thinking about not owning a suit the other day . . ."

"Did you?"

"I did. And I got to thinking that if I were to want to go to a party with you, I'd have to own a suit."

She began to ask him a question, then stopped and waited, but when he didn't continue, she said, "And?"

"And so I went out the other day and bought something."

She felt a smile teasing her lips, but she held it back, not entirely certain what was coming. "And?"

"And what I bought was a suit."

"Oh, Grady!" She blinked back tears, shaking her head back and forth.

He nodded. "Now, I don't want you to get the wrong idea, Jennie."

"Don't you?" she whispered.

"No. But I did buy this suit, which I thought I'd wear to your party tomorrow night. If you want me to come with you, that is."

"Grady," she murmured, sliding her arms around his neck, "have I told you that you're a wonderful man?"

He grinned down at her, tightening his hold. "I do believe you have."

"And have I told you that I love you as much as the universe is big?"

"I do believe you have. And, I might add, you're not very original."

"Yeah," she whispered, pulling his head down to hers. "But what I lack in originality, I make up for in ardor."

He grinned, then caught her up against him, swinging her around and around. "Yeah, and I'll take ardor any day. . . ."

TELL US YOUR OPINIONS AND RECEIVE A FREE COPY OF THE RAPTURE NEWSLETTER.

Thank you for filling out our questionnaire. Your response to the following questions will help us to bring you more and better books. In appreciation of your help we will send you a free copy of the Rapture Newsletter.

1. Book Title:_____

   Book # :_____ (5–7)

2. Using the scale below how would you rate this book on the following features? Please write in one rating from 0–10 for each feature in the spaces provided. Ignore bracketed numbers.

(Poor) 0 1 2 3 4 5 6 7 8 9 10 (Excellent)
                                                    0–10 Rating

Overall Opinion of Book. . . . . . . . . . . . . . . . . _____ (8)
Plot/Story. . . . . . . . . . . . . . . . . . . . . . . . . _____ (9)
Setting/Location. . . . . . . . . . . . . . . . . . . . . _____ (10)
Writing Style. . . . . . . . . . . . . . . . . . . . . . . _____ (11)
Dialogue. . . . . . . . . . . . . . . . . . . . . . . . . . _____ (12)
Love Scenes. . . . . . . . . . . . . . . . . . . . . . . . _____ (13)
Character Development:
Heroine:. . . . . . . . . . . . . . . . . . . . . . . . . . . _____ (14)
Hero:. . . . . . . . . . . . . . . . . . . . . . . . . . . . . _____ (15)
Romantic Scene on Front Cover. . . . . . . . . . _____ (16)
Back Cover Story Outline . . . . . . . . . . . . . . _____ (17)
First Page Excerpts. . . . . . . . . . . . . . . . . . . _____ (18)

3. What is your: Education:    Age:_____(20-22)

     High School  (   )1    4 Yrs. College (   )3
     2 Yrs. College (   )2    Post Grad     (   )4 (23)

4. Print Name:_____

   Address:_____

   City:_____State:_____Zip:_____

   Phone # (      )_____ (25)

Thank you for your time and effort. Please send to New American Library, Rapture Romance Research Department, 1633 Broadway, New York, NY 10019.

# GET SIX RAPTURE ROMANCES EVERY MONTH FOR THE PRICE OF FIVE.

**Subscribe to Rapture Romance and every month you'll get six new books for the price of five.** That's an $11.70 value for just $9.75. We're so sure you'll love them, we'll give you 10 days to look them over at home. Then you can keep all six and pay for only five, or return the books and owe nothing.

**To start you off, we'll send you four books absolutely FREE.** "Apache Tears," "Love's Gilded Mask," "O'Hara's Woman," and "Love So Fearful." The total value of all four books is $7.80, but they're yours *free* even if you never buy another book.

So order Rapture Romances today. And prepare to meet a different breed of man.

# YOUR FIRST 4 BOOKS ARE FREE!
# JUST PHONE 1-800-228-1888*

(Or mail the coupon below)
*In Nebraska call 1-800-642-8788

-------------------------------------------------

**Rapture Romance, P.O. Box 996, Greens Farms, CT 06436**

Please send me the 4 Rapture Romances described in this ad FREE and without obligation. Unless you hear from me after I receive them, send me 6 NEW Rapture Romances to preview each month. I understand that you will bill me for only 5 of them at $1.95 each (a total of $9.75) with no shipping, handling or other charges. I always get one book FREE every month. There is no minimum number of books I must buy, and I can cancel at any time. The first 4 FREE books are mine to keep even if I never buy another book.

| | |
|---|---|
| Name | (please print) |

| | |
|---|---|
| Address | City |

| | | |
|---|---|---|
| State | Zip | Signature (if under 18, parent or guardian must sign) |

 RAPTURE ROMANCE

This offer, limited to one per household and not valid to present subscribers, expires June 30, 1984. Prices subject to change. Specific titles subject to availability. Allow a minimum of 4 weeks for delivery.

RR 183

# RAPTURE ROMANCE

**Provocative and sensual,
passionate and tender—
the magic and mystery of love
in all its many guises**

## Coming next month

**A DISTANT LIGHT by Ellie Winslow.** As suddenly as he'd once disappeared, Louis Dupierre reentered Tara's life. Was it the promise of ecstasy, or some unknown, darker reason that brought him back? Tara didn't know, nor was she sure whether she could risk loving—and trusting—Louis again . . .

**PASSIONATE ENTERPRISE by Charlotte Wisely.** Gwen Franklin's business sense surrendered to sensual pleasure in the arms of executive Kurt Jensen. But could Gwen keep working to prove she could rise as high as any man in the corporate world—when she was falling so deeply in love?

**TORRENT OF LOVE by Marianna Essex.** By day, architect Erin Kelly struggled against arrogant builder Alex Butler, but at night, their lovemaking was sheer ecstasy. Yet when their project ended, so did their affair, and Erin was struggling again—to make Alex see beyond business, into her heart . . .

**LOVE'S JOURNEY HOME by Bree Thomas.** Soap opera star Katherine Ransom was back home—and back in the arms of Joe Mercer, the man who'd once stolen her heart. But caught up in irresistible passion, Katherine soon found herself forced to choose between her glamorous career— and Joe . . .

**AMBER DREAMS by Diana Morgan.** Jenny Moffatt was determined to overcome Ryan Powers and his big money interests. But instead, his incredible attractiveness awed her, and she was swept away by desire . . .

**WINTER FLAME by Deborah Benét.** Darcy had vowed never to see Chason again. But now her ex-husband was back, conquering her with loving caresses. If Chason wanted to reestablish their marriage, would his love be enough to help her overcome the past. . . ?

# RAPTURE ROMANCE

### Provocative and sensual, passionate and tender— the magic and mystery of love in all its many guises

### NEW Titles Available Now

(0451)

**#33☐APACHE TEARS by Marianne Clark.** Navajo Adam Hawk willingly taught Catriona Frazer his secrets of silversmithing while together they learned the art of love. But was their passion enough to overcome the prejudices of their different cultures?(125525—$1.95)*

**#34☐AGAINST ALL ODDS by Leslie Morgan.** Editorial cartoonist Jennifer Aldrich scorned all politicians—before she met Ben Trostel. But love and politics didn't mix, and Jennifer had to choose which she wanted more: her job or Ben . . . . (122533—$1.95)*

**#35☐UNTAMED DESIRE by Kasey Adams.** Lacy Barnett vowed ruthless land tycoon Ward Blaine would never possess her. But he wore down her resistance with the same gentleness and strength he used to saddle-break the proudest steed . . . until Lacy wasn't fighting his desire, but her own . . . (125541—$1.95)*

**#36☐LOVE'S GILDED MASK by Francine Shore.** A painful divorce made Merilyn swear never again to let any man break through her defenses. Then she met Morgan Drake. . . . (122568—$1.95)*

**#37☐O'HARA'S WOMAN by Katherine Ransom.** Grady O'Hara had long ago abandoned the high-powered executive life that Jennie Winters seemed to thrive on. Could she sacrifice her career for his love—and would she be happy if she did? (122576—$1.95)*

**#38☐HEART ON TRIAL by Tricia Graves.** Janelle Taylor wasn't going to let anyone come between her and her law career. But her rival, attorney Blair Wynter, was equally determined to get his way opposite her in the courtroom—and the bedroom . . . (122584—$1.95)*

*Price is $2.25 in Canada

To order, use coupon on next page

# RAPTURE ROMANCE

### Provocative and sensual, passionate and tender— the magic and mystery of love in all its many guises

---

Buy them at your local bookstore or use this convenient coupon for ordering.
**THE NEW AMERICAN LIBRARY, INC.**
**P.O. Box 999, Bergenfield, New Jersey 07621**
Please send me the books I have checked above. I am enclosing $_____
(please add $1.00 to this order to cover postage and handling). Send check
or money order—no cash or C.O.D.'s. Prices and numbers are subject to change
without notice.
Name_____
Address_____
City _____ State _____ Zip Code _____
Allow 4-6 weeks for delivery.
This offer is subject to withdrawal without notice.

# SPECIAL $1.00 REBATE OFFER
# WHEN YOU BUY
# FOUR RAPTURE ROMANCES

To receive your cash refund, send:

1. This coupon: To qualify for the $1.00 refund, this coupon, completed with your name and address, must be used. (Certificate may not be reproduced)

2. Proof of purchase: Print, on the reverse side of this coupon, the *title* of the books, the *numbers* of the books (on the upper right hand of the front cover preceding the price), and the U.P.C. numbers (on the back covers) on your next four purchases.

3. Cash register receipts, with prices circled to:
   Rapture Romance $1.00 Refund Offer
   P.O. Box NB037
   El Paso, Texas 79977

Offer good only in the U.S. and Canada. Limit one refund/response per household for any group of four Rapture Romance titles. Void where prohibited, taxed or restricted. Allow 6–8 weeks for delivery. Offer expires March 31, 1984.

NAME_____

ADDRESS_____

CITY_____STATE_____ZIP_____

# SPECIAL $1.00 REBATE OFFER
# WHEN YOU BUY
# FOUR RAPTURE ROMANCES

See complete details on reverse

1. Book Title _____

   Book Number 451-_____

   U.P.C. Number 7116200195-_____

2. Book Title _____

   Book Number 451-_____

   U.P.C. Number 7116200195-_____

3. Book Title _____

   Book Number 451-_____

   U.P.C. Number 7116200195-_____

4. Book Title _____

   Book Number 451-_____

   U.P.C. Number 7116200195-_____

U.P.C. Number

SAMPLE

0   71162 00195